SWEET MEMORIES

NICOLE ELLIS

1

"*A*ngel, did you finish the éclairs?"

Angel Bennett looked up from the recipe she was studying and smiled. Her boss, Maggie Price, was staring down at her with her face flushed and wisps of hair poking out of her ponytail as though she'd just run a mile uphill.

"I did." She pointed to an immaculate countertop in the corner of the Bluebonnet Café's kitchen, which held four neat rows of a dozen chocolate iced éclairs each.

Maggie sighed and a relieved smile spread across her lips. "Thank goodness. The Ladies of Candle Beach are here this morning for their weekly breakfast meeting and I don't know what they'd do if we didn't have their standing order of éclairs ready for them. I'll have someone bring them out to their table."

Angel laughed. "I know. Last week I didn't have them quite ready when they arrived and Agnes Barnes came into the kitchen to give me a talking to." The Ladies, as they called themselves, were a group of elderly women who thought they owned the town of Candle Beach. Truth was,

I

they probably did, or knew people that did. She tilted her head up to regard Maggie more closely. "Are you okay? You look stressed."

"Oh, sure. I'm fine." Maggie brushed the errant strands of hair back from her face. "I've just been running around like a chicken with my head cut off this morning. With the remodeling of the new event venue out at the Sorensen Farm and everything here and at home, I haven't had much of a chance to relax."

Angel narrowed her eyes at Maggie. Although she'd only known her for about a month, she'd come to respect her boss and considered her a friend. "You need to take better care of yourself."

"I know. But that will have to wait until I get the barn remodeled for the Sweethearts' Dance next month."

"Is that on Valentine's Day?"

Maggie nodded. "Yes. I don't think we'll have everything done, but a barn dance is supposed to be rustic, right?"

"Right." Angel grinned and shook her head. A barn dance? Life on the Washington coast was a far cry from the big city life she'd left behind in Southern California.

"Now, how is the new chocolate soufflé recipe coming?" Maggie pointed at the recipe card, which had whole sections scribbled out. "I see you've been making some adjustments."

"I'm tweaking it a little. It should be ready by tomorrow." She checked the clock. "But I've got to get the muffins done first." She hopped off the stool and walked over to the baking counter.

"I'll let you get to it." Maggie scurried off in the direction of her office, her wavy red hair streaming out behind her in a long ponytail.

Angel sifted flour and combined it with sugar and other

ingredients to make the café's famous blueberry muffins. She eyed the lengthy baking to-do list on the wall. This was going to take a while.

She poured the blueberry-studded batter into the deep wells of the giant muffin tins and sprinkled coarse raw sugar crystals over the top before placing them in the oven. When that was finished, she washed her hands off and started on the next task.

Back in Los Angeles, she'd attended college and then culinary school before working at an up-and-coming dessert shop until her mother had become extremely sick. After her mother died, she'd quit her job on impulse and moved to Candle Beach. Luckily for her, the Bluebonnet Café had been in dire need of a new pastry chef and Maggie had hired her on the spot. She had seen Angel's potential and given her more responsibility than Angel had expected.

The job kept her so busy that she'd put off pursuing the reason she'd moved thousands of miles away from everything she knew. At least that was what she told herself. With a twinge in her stomach, she glanced at the staff lockers where she'd stored her cell phone and purse.

"Angel!" Elvin, the assistant manager, called to her from the kitchen doorway. "A huge group just came in and we need your help in the front."

She checked the timer on the oven. Four minutes left. "I'll be right there after I get the muffins out of the oven."

He nodded and left.

The timer dinged and Angel pulled the muffin tins out of the oven, the heat blasting her face. After setting them on the cooling racks, she brushed off her hands and took a quick look at her apron. It was covered with flour—not a great look for customer service work. She hung the apron on a hook by the door and went out to the front to help at the register.

With the dishwasher running, the griddle sizzling and pots clanging in the kitchen, she hadn't heard the din of the crowd in the lobby, but now she could see why they needed her help. A line of hungry customers snaked all the way outside and a cool breezed drafted through the lobby from the open door. She shivered and hugged her arms to her chest. As always, the kitchen had been warm, but out here, the January cold was apparent.

Maggie stood in front of the register, calmly handing change to a customer, but her eyes held a frantic gleam.

"If you can get the to-go coffee orders, that would be a huge help. I've marked them with each person's name to make it easier." Maggie nodded at the pastry case and a row of labeled paper to-go cups on the glass top, and then smoothly returned to helping customers.

"Sure, no problem." Angel grabbed the first two cups and filled them with freshly brewed coffee, then placed the customer's pastry order in a white paper bag before calling the name printed on the cup.

Forty-five minutes later, and only a few drink order mix-ups, the afternoon rush was finally over.

"Well, now that the whole town is caffeinated, I guess I can get back to baking," she joked.

"I'm sorry, Angel." Maggie's lips turned downward. "I didn't mean to take you away from your baking for so long. I can help you if you'd like?"

"No, that's fine." Angel smiled at her. "I don't have any plans, so I can stay late today. Besides, you've got enough on your plate."

Relief passed across Maggie's face. "Thanks. I knew I

made the right choice when I hired you. I don't know what we'd do without you."

Angel swelled with pride. Even if she had no family in town, Maggie had made sure she felt welcome there by finding her lodging and introducing her to her own friends. In L.A., she'd been so focused on work that she hadn't had much time for friends, so she was enjoying her time in Candle Beach, for however long it might be.

"So are you going to go to the Sweethearts' Dance?" Maggie asked while cracking open a new roll of quarters and depositing them in the till.

"Haha." Angel made a face.

"What?" Maggie said. "It'll be fun."

"I don't exactly have a sweetheart. I barely know anyone in town." She used a rag to mop up a small spot of spilled coffee on the counter.

"Oh, that." Maggie waved her hand in the air. "It's just a name. You don't even need a date at all. The Sweethearts' Dance has been a Candle Beach tradition for over fifty years. Before I had the Sorensen Farm, it was held in the school gym. This year is going to blow all the other years out of the water."

Angel thought about it. Since coming to town, she hadn't done much of anything but go from work to home and back. A trip to the grocery store was the highlight of her week.

"I'll think about it." Even though Maggie had said a date wasn't required, it felt weird to think of going to a couples dance without a significant other.

"Great!" Maggie hugged her around the shoulders with one arm.

"Do you need help getting the farm ready for the dance?"

Maggie hesitated. "Yes, but I couldn't ask you to do that."

"Maggie. Do you know how much you've done for me?" Not only had she given Angel a job when she was practically penniless, she'd found her a place to live over her friend's garage.

Maggie waved her hand in the air across her body. "Oh, that was nothing. Anyone here would have helped."

"Not back home they wouldn't have." She frowned. Everything was so hectic in the city that people could barely remember a new person's name, much less find them a place to live.

"Well, you're here now and we take care of our own, okay?" Maggie smiled warmly at her. The regular cashier rushed in and relieved Maggie from her post behind the register.

Angel smiled at Maggie. "Thanks, though. I appreciate everything you've done for me."

"Don't even worry about it. I've got to run, but check in with me later. I think Jake is organizing a work party next week out at the farm."

"I'll see you after my shift." Angel grabbed her apron from the hook and tied it at her waist. Being out front wasn't as bad as she'd thought it would be, but now she was ready to get back to doing what she loved.

Maggie nodded and returned to her office.

Angel retreated to her corner of the kitchen, her own little oasis set apart from the hustle and bustle of the grill and swinging door into the restaurant's main dining area. She checked the baking list and pulled out the ingredients for the giant chocolate chip cookies that the customers couldn't get enough of. She'd now made them so many times that she could bake them on autopilot, which gave her too much time to think.

It had been a while since she'd dated anyone, much less

had anyone that came close to being a serious sweetheart. Maggie had recently become engaged to Jake, a man she'd known for many years, but hadn't dated for long. Anyone with eyes could see that they were meant for each other and Angel had been rooting for them to be a couple as much as everyone else in town had. It was amazing how quickly things worked out when two people were destined for each other. Although she was happy for Maggie, she sometimes wondered if she would ever find the same happiness.

She shook her head. Now wasn't the time. Finding her soul mate wasn't the reason she was in Candle Beach. With the cookies in the oven, she made her way across the crowded kitchen to her locker. Her fingers trembled as she twisted the combination lock. When it clicked open, she glanced furtively around the room to see if anyone was looking. Everyone was engrossed in their own roles.

From her purse, she pulled out a Polaroid photo of a family standing in front of a white house. The photo was yellowed with age, but she knew it was the same house she remembered from a long-ago memory of Candle Beach. She'd finally worked up the nerve to search for the house, but with the short winter days, there likely wouldn't be enough light left after work to see anything, much less look for a house that she wasn't even sure existed. Still, maybe if she got out on time, she'd be able to do some reconnaissance.

∼

When Angel pushed open the back door to the café after her shift was over, the streetlights were shining brightly and the sky was dark. Looking for the white house would have to wait for another day. She crossed through the alley to the sidewalk on Main Street, stuffing her hands in her coat pockets. In front of her, a happy couple swung their arms between them as they chatted, and she stepped aside to allow them room to pass without breaking their connection. A family with two small children darted across the street at the four-way stop's crosswalk and headed toward the Chinese restaurant on the other side.

Angel stared wistfully at the children giggling as they skipped across. What would it be like to have a brother or sister? Growing up, she'd always wished for a large family, but it had just been her and her mother for most of her childhood. That house in the picture may be the answer to her prayers—if only she could locate it. She pushed the frustration out of her head and climbed the hill above town to the studio apartment she was renting over Maggie's friend Gretchen's garage. When the beautiful robin's egg blue Craftsman home Gretchen lived in came into view, she hiked down a side street to the alley.

At the top of the carriage house stairs, she stopped and tilted her head to the side to take in the peek-a-boo view to the west. The Pacific Ocean below was illuminated by the moon, its angry waves pounding against the sand. Everything about this place was so different from the sunny locale where she'd grown up. Winter weather specifically was taking some getting used to.

She'd come to Candle Beach to find out who her family was, but every time she thought she was ready to find them, she lost her nerve. Whenever Angel had asked her mother about where she'd grown up, Erin Bennett had shut down. After she'd died last year, Angel had discovered the photo of her mother as a teenager standing in front of a white house, alongside a slightly younger girl and a couple she assumed was their parents. On the back, in her mother's loopy handwriting, were the words *Candle Beach, 1986*.

However, the old photo was all Angel had to go on—she didn't even know her mother's maiden name. While her stepfather had been a nice man, he and her mom hadn't had any more children and Angel had desperately wished for a brother or sister. Every time she'd seen kids playing with their siblings, she'd felt a pang of envy.

Work had been busy since she arrived in town and she'd allowed herself to believe she didn't have time to find out anything about her mother. She was scared. Dreaming about them was one thing, but what if her grandparents were still alive and they didn't want anything to do with her? Or worse yet, what if she had no family left in Candle Beach?

Her mother had never spoken of her parents, so they could be monsters for all she knew. Considering the lack of contact between her mother and them, they probably wanted nothing to do with their daughter and granddaughter. But was it better to find that out for certain than to wonder about them for the rest of her life?

She couldn't keep thinking about it and doing nothing. Before unlocking the front door, she pivoted and hurried back down the steps toward her car. She knew if she stopped to think about it, she'd chicken out. Once inside the car, she gripped the top of the wheel and rested her head on her hands. Her need to find her family had risen to the top and she couldn't suppress it any longer. Looking for the white house couldn't wait for another day.

Why was she doing this? There was very little chance she could find the house in the dark. But she couldn't live with herself if she lost another day when she could have searched for her family. The fear that had kept her back now ate away at her, increasing the emotional pressure until she couldn't procrastinate any longer. Even if she found them and they were indeed monsters, at least she'd know.

She turned the key, and the engine of her sporty Honda roared to life. Carefully, she drove down the hill and made her way up and down some of the streets she'd identified as areas that contained houses of the same era as the one in the photo. The houses in these neighborhoods were older, but well taken care of, with well-manicured lawns, even in the dead of winter. It was possible that the family picture had been taken somewhere other than in front of their own home, but the house looked vaguely familiar to her, as if she had seen it herself as a child. Plus, it was the only lead she had.

One house on Elm Street resembled the house in the picture, so she stopped the car. Hugging her coat tightly to her body, she stepped out onto the sidewalk and stared at the house. It was so cold that her breath formed puffy clouds that dissipated like wisps of smoke into the night air.

From the glow of her headlights and the street lamp, she could see most of the exterior of the house, although the porch light was off. It was now painted yellow, but the windows and door were in the right place. It didn't look exactly the same though. How could she find out if this was the right place? What was she supposed to do, knock on the door and ask if they knew her mother?

If she stayed here staring at their house, pretty soon the residents would think she was stalking them. She shook her head. The only thing she could do at this time was to guess about whether or not it was the house in the photo. Still, she wrote down the address and street name for later.

With her head hung low, she retreated to her car, taking one last look at the house through the passenger side window before she returned to her apartment. The lights were on in Gretchen's house, and through the sheer drapes she could see two silhouettes dancing and laughing—most likely Gretchen and her boyfriend Parker. She wanted that —someone who loved her and made her feel safe. Having someone to dance with on a cold winter night seemed a far-off prospect at the moment.

Her heart ached as she entered the apartment and drew the drapes closed, ostensibly to keep out the cold, but it had the convenient effect of blocking the view of Gretchen's house as well. Plopping down on the loveseat, she put her feet up on the coffee table and stared at the blank wall. If that had been the correct house, what was the next step? She knew very few people in town, but Maggie seemed like a logical person to ask. She'd lived in Candle Beach for most of her life and had connections around town. Angel resolved to ask her for advice the next day.

With that decided, she flipped on the TV, microwaved some dinner, and curled up with a blanket alone on the loveseat. If she was going to stay in Candle Beach much longer, she needed to get a pet. Her studio apartment wasn't huge, but it felt awfully lonely living there by herself.

"*I*'m sorry, Adam, but we can't give you the loan."

Lars Johnson looked up at him with a kindly smile. "There's just not enough evidence that a web presence for the *Candle Beach Weekly* would increase profits enough to pay the money back. If circumstances change, please let us know. I'd love to be able to help you and this community needs their newspaper." He nodded to a copy of the *Weekly* on his desk. "I know I do." He smiled again, then stacked the papers in a neat pile and placed them in front of Adam. Then, he pushed back his leather desk chair and stood, straightening his charcoal gray pin-striped suit.

That would be the cue to leave. Adam Rigg smiled and stood too, shaking Lars's hand. "I understand. Thank you for considering my application."

He picked up his business plan from the desk and walked slowly through the bank. The leather soles of his shoes tapped against the marble floor. It felt as though everyone's eyes were on him, although most likely they were all engrossed in their own bank transactions. He greeted a few of the customers then pushed on the glass door, stepping out into the sunny but chilly-to-the-bone January afternoon.

Now what? When he'd bought the *Candle Beach Weekly* from its octogenarian owner a few years prior, sales had been in the dumps and ad revenues had been almost nonexistent. He'd improved the business to the point where it was currently self-sustaining, but lately, the lack of new subscriptions and dwindling sales had caused concerns about the newspaper's future. To bring it into the twenty-first century, the newspaper would have to have a web presence to increase ad revenues. However, having a website designed and maintained would cost more than he could afford at the moment.

But now that he'd been turned down for a loan by the only bank in Candle Beach, how was he going to get the money to make the necessary improvements?

He walked away from the bank in a daze, heading down Main Street. Halfway to the newspaper office, someone touched him on the arm.

"Hey," a woman said. She had her arm linked with that of a tall, handsome man.

He looked up and sadness pinged through his chest. Gretchen Roberts and her boyfriend, Parker Gray. She smiled up at Adam, then adjusted the turquoise crocheted winter hat she wore over her long dark hair. Her face was flushed prettily from the cold and she looked as adorable now as she had when they were kids, sledding together down Main Street on a snowy day off from school.

"Hey, Gretchen. Parker. Nice to see you."

She peered at him, scrutinizing his face. "Are you okay? You look like you're on autopilot."

Next to her, Parker shifted on his feet and stared off toward the park. Adam followed his gaze. Children's laughter floated out from the swings as they soared higher and higher into the sky. Near the playset, their mothers sat on wooden benches, clutching warm cups of to-go coffee from the Bluebonnet Café as they chatted with each other.

He forced a smile. "I'm fine. I was meeting with Lars Johnson at the bank. I've got to get going though, I hope you both enjoy the beautiful day."

"Wait. You don't look okay. What's wrong?"

He shot a glance at Parker. "I can tell you some other time, it looks like you two are on your way to somewhere."

"Okay," she said, but the concern on her face remained. "I'll give you a call later. It's been a while since we had a chance to catch up. Parker and I are making progress on our new real estate company. I'll be sure to hit you up for some ads in the paper when we open for business."

"Sure. That would be great."

He waved at them and continued his trek down the hill. Gravel on the pavement crunched under the wing tip shoes he'd worn with his suit for the meeting at the bank. He loosened his tie with one hand. The darn things always made his throat feel like someone was choking him. As soon as he was back at the office, he'd change into the cotton polo shirt and khaki pants that he wore almost like a uniform at work.

A block later, he stopped to look back behind him. Gretchen and Parker were walking hand in hand away from him, toward the Bluebonnet Café. As he watched, Parker must have said something funny, because Gretchen stopped and laughed before gently slugging his arm and kissing him on the cheek.

Adam swallowed a knot in his throat that hadn't been caused by the boa-constrictor-like tie. He dropped off his business plan on his desk at the newspaper office, and then went upstairs to his small one-bedroom apartment.

A cold, wet nose greeted him at the door.

"Hey, Otis." He leaned down to pet the shaggy golden retriever. Otis rewarded him by nudging against his leg.

"You probably want to go out, huh?" Adam said to the dog. Otis heard "out" and tried to squeeze past his owner, almost bowling Adam over in the process.

"Hold on buddy, I've got to change my clothes." At least his dog was glad to see him, and a walk would do both of them good.

He changed out of his clothes, carefully re-hanging his suit in its garment bag and placing it in the back of the closet so it would be ready for the next time he had to be formally dressed.

After checking to make sure he had transferred everything from his suit pockets, he hooked the leash onto Otis's collar and pulled his apartment door shut. Otis galloped down the stairs and it was all Adam could do to keep up with him. Normally, they would go for a long walk in the mornings or play in the park, but Adam had been too preoccupied that morning to do more than let him out for a few minutes. He followed Otis to the newspaper office's front door and locked it behind him.

The dog instinctively tugged at the leash, pulling him down the hill past Candle Beach Kids and the Seaside Grill, and not stopping until they'd reached the top of the beach trail that overlooked the ocean. Below him, the Pacific Ocean roared with the force of a freight train, its waves leaving foam along the shore for the birds to traverse as they hunted for something tasty to eat.

He breathed in the cold, salty air and willed his body to relax. He'd grown up in Candle Beach and had worked as a delivery boy for the *Candle Beach Weekly* as a child. It had always been his dream to own the newspaper, a dream that had come true via hard work and discipline. Now, it could all be in jeopardy if he couldn't modernize its operations. Every other paper in the coastal region had an online presence. Subscriptions had dropped lately as more and more people got their news online and he needed to keep up with the times. At this rate, he'd be out of business within a year.

Otis tugged on the leash, eager to get down to the sand. Adam took another deep breath and climbed down the steep stairs to the beach. Lately, nothing seemed to be going right. Seeing Gretchen and Parker together had hurt more than he'd wanted to admit. He and Gretchen had been childhood friends, and in the back of his mind he'd always thought they'd end up together. After a disastrous date last summer, he'd realized that prospect was unlikely, and now seeing her so happy with Parker, he knew with certainty that they'd never be more than friends.

It didn't really matter though. He didn't have time for a relationship—not if he wanted to make the newspaper a success and a viable business for the future. When he was in college, he'd allowed his emotions to take control and he'd lost out on a prestigious job to stay in Washington, D.C. while his college girlfriend finished up school. But he couldn't afford anything like that now. This was real life, and his savings wouldn't keep the newspaper afloat much longer.

Seagulls scattered as he and Otis walked along the edge of the water on the hard-packed sand. Few people were out on the beach, but those who braved the cold were bundled up in heavy jackets. He stuffed his hands in his own coat pockets, rubbing his thumbs and fingers together to warm them. It was time to get to work. News on the coast had been slow lately, but he needed to drum up something to keep his subscribers informed and entertained.

A little kid, probably about four years old, splashed around in the tide pools in his rubber boots while his mother urged him not to get too wet. The kid jumped in a large puddle, spraying water everywhere, then looked at his mother in defiance. Adam had to stifle a grin. His little niece would do exactly the same thing.

He checked his watch. They'd been out for over an hour and he really needed to get back to work.

"Hey old buddy, time to go home." He tugged on the leash and pointed up the hill toward town.

If there was a dog pout Olympics, Otis would be a champion.

Adam grinned at the comical expression on his dog's face. "Sorry. We'll go out later, I promise."

A couple walking past gave him an odd look, most likely because they'd heard him talking to his dog. He smiled and waved at the strangers. Their lips slipped into polite smiles as they hurried past them. *Great.* He was supposed to be convincing tourists that Candle Beach was a wonderful place to visit and now this couple thought it was full of loonies. He and Otis hiked back up the hill. Upon entering the apartment, the dog walked over to a rug near the kitchen and lay down, no doubt to pout some more. Adam returned to work downstairs, intent on researching a new story he was working on about the logging industry's plans for the area.

He'd persuaded a local landowner, John Nichols, to speak with him about a prospective sale of his trees to a nearby lumber mill. Although Nichols was normally reluctant to discuss anything with the media, Adam had finally worn him down and they'd scheduled a meeting for next week. If he played his cards right, he could get a scoop on things before all of the other coastal newspapers. A story like that could influence new people to subscribe to the *Weekly*, but first he needed to make sure he was up to date on everything regarding the logging industry.

He signed on to his computer and started the immense task in front of him. His love life may never recover from being in a shambles, but at least he was doing everything he could to make the paper a success.

3

*A*fter a fruitless day off work spent searching the rest of town for any other houses that resembled the one in the photo, Angel gave up. She'd revisited the house she'd seen on Elm Street and it was the closest she'd found to the one in the photo. But, she still didn't know who owned it. Being new to town, she was pretty clueless about how things like that worked. Now back at the café the next day, she couldn't get it out of her mind, which wasn't helping her limited customer service skills.

"Angel," Maggie said sharply, waving her hand in front of Angel's face. "Can you please warm up a chocolate muffin for this customer?"

"What?" Angel said without thinking.

Maggie arched her eyebrows. "You must have been pretty far away. Mr. Duggins would like a warm chocolate muffin and a large cup of coffee to go."

Angel blushed. "Sorry, Maggie." She smiled apologetically at the customer. "I'll have it up for you in a minute." She grabbed a dark muffin out of the case with the tongs and stuck it in the warmer while pouring him a cup of coffee. When the timer dinged she pulled the muffin out, expecting to see warm chocolate chips melting into a cocoa-filled muffin. However, when she opened the oven, the distinct scent of heated bran assaulted her nose.

Well, that's what you get when you aren't paying attention. She glanced at the customer and put it onto a plate, sliding it behind a tall coffee carafe on the back counter. The customer had his nose in a newspaper, so she quickly snuck over to the glass bakery case and removed the correct type of muffin. When it was warmed, she called out, "chocolate muffin and coffee to go" and handed it to the customer, who was none the wiser.

Her next customer, an elderly woman, walked up to the counter, smiling happily at Angel as she accepted her coffee and baked treat. With a start, Angel realized that this could be her grandmother. Chances were that it wasn't, but it could be. Candle Beach was a small town and she may have already met members of her family and not even have known it. A chill shot through her. With each order, she examined the customer, wondering if it could be someone she was related to.

She and Maggie worked together to get through the line until Maggie said, "I've got to go pick up my son from school. They've got another half-day today." She eyed the growing line. "Are you going to be okay up here by yourself? Anna was having some car trouble, but she should be in soon to relieve you."

"Of course I'll be fine." Angel gave her a reassuring smile, even though the idea of being left alone made her stomach flip-flop. Now she really needed to focus on what she was doing and put any thoughts of her family out of her mind for the meantime. "Go. Don't worry about me."

Maggie hesitated as if she was about to say something,

but instead removed her apron and exited the lobby to the kitchen.

A new group of customers came in and Angel was busy for a while helping them. It got to the point where she barely saw who she was helping, but instead became a pouring-and-warming machine taking people's money.

"Busy today, isn't it?" a man's voice asked.

"Yes, it is. What can I get you?" Angel held her fingers above the cash register keys, ready to calculate his order.

"Oh, maybe one of those purple roosters I saw out on the sidewalk."

Her head shot up. Had she heard him correctly? "Excuse me?"

A grin spread across his freckled face. "I wanted to see if you were a robot. You've been breezing through every order, but I don't think you've seen anyone."

She laughed. "You're right." The line had dwindled and she took the opportunity to take a deep breath. "I'm not usually up front, so I'm not as good at multitasking as Maggie and the others are."

"Ah," he said. "I thought I didn't recognize you. I know most of the people in town."

"I just moved to Candle Beach last month," she explained. She'd never seen him before either, although that wasn't much of a surprise considering how little she got out of the house. His friendly, Dennis the Menace face and carrot-red hair made her feel instantly at ease.

He nodded and glanced at her name tag. "Well, nice to meet you, Angel. I hope you're enjoying life in our little town."

"I am." She grinned. "Now, what can I get you?"

He pointed at the top shelf of the domed bakery case. "I've been eyeing that last cherry Danish. I was really worried the man in front of me was going to take it when he ordered a dozen pastries. They're my favorite and I'm not usually in here early enough to get one. This is my lucky day." He grinned from ear to ear.

"Yes, fortunately for you, he was more of a chocolate croissant fan." She tapped his order into the cash register and told him his total.

He rummaged in his wallet and pulled out a few crumpled dollar bills, holding them out to her. When she reached for the money, their hands touched briefly—just long enough for threads of attraction to shoot through his fingertips to hers. Their eyes met and he smiled at her.

She pulled her fingers away as if burned by his touch, and made a show of calmly putting the bills in the register before pushing his change across the counter to him. What was going on? She didn't spend much time at the cash register, but she definitely hadn't felt that sensation with any other customer before.

Hiding her face in the pastry case, she picked up the Danish and placed it carefully in a white paper bag.

"Here you go," she said, holding it out to him, determined not to let her emotions get the best of her.

His hand grazed hers and she let go of the bag in surprise. They both watched as it dropped from her hands, almost as if watching a movie in slow motion.

"Oh no!" Her eyes widened and she leaned over the counter. "I'm sorry."

The man fumbled trying to grab it, causing the white bag to fall to the floor, upended. She stared in horror as the pastry slid out of the bag onto the tile floor of the café lobby.

The Danish broke in half upon impact and the fruit center oozed onto the floor. He stared sadly at his mangled breakfast.

"Oh, I'm so sorry," Angel whispered, her eyes locked on it as well.

"That was the last one," he said, glancing at the case, as if hoping another would have magically appeared.

Her face flushed with heat and her gaze darted to the pastry case. It had indeed been the last cherry Danish. And he'd been so excited to get it. Acid churned in her stomach. He seemed nice, but something like this could make anyone grouchy and she'd assured Maggie that everything would go smoothly while she was gone.

"Is there something else I can get you? I know you wanted the Danish, but the butter tarts I made this morning are excellent too." She picked up the tongs and waited. *Please, please let him not be upset.*

He brought his attention to her face and swept his hand in front of the glass display case. "You made all of these? Maggie's always had great baked goods at the café, but I'd noticed they were even better than usual lately. That was you?"

He wasn't mad. She let out the breath she hadn't known she'd been holding and nodded. "I follow Maggie's recipes though. Well, for the most part. I'm glad you like them." She motioned to the pastries. "Is there something I can get you instead of the Danish? I feel really bad about ruining your breakfast."

He waved his hand. "Don't worry about it. I'm sure I'll love anything you made." He checked the selection. "You know, I think I will go with the butter tart. It looks delicious."

From behind him, a woman cleared her throat. "Miss, I'd like to order." She jangled her keys and eyed the clock behind the counter.

Flustered, Angel said, "I'll be right with you, ma'am."

She placed a butter tart in a white paper bag, just as she'd done before with the cherry Danish, but this time, she folded over the edge to seal the bag—just in case. She handed it to the man.

"Thank you," he said. "Maybe there will be more Danishes tomorrow?" He gave her a sad, puppy-dog look that endeared him to her immediately.

She laughed. "There will be, even if I have to come in extra early to make them."

He gave her a thumbs-up. "I'll be here." He turned to walk away.

"Hey," she called after him. "Give me your name and I'll save one for you tomorrow."

He opened his mouth to answer, but his words were drowned out by the loud order from the woman who'd been waiting behind him. Seeming not to notice she hadn't heard, he wove his way through the crowd and left.

She shrugged. She'd leave a cherry Danish out for him and hope he got it. There was something about the mystery man that made her want to know more about him. Maybe it was the cheerful way he joked with her or his cute, friendly face. Or maybe it was that surprising sensation that had warmed her fingertips when their hands met.

"Miss," the woman at the head of the line said insistently. "My coffee?"

She forced herself to pay attention. "Sorry, ma'am."

The woman harrumphed and Angel turned to get her order. Hopefully Maggie would be back soon and she could retreat to her haven of baking back in the kitchen. She didn't think she was cut out for dealing with customers on a long-term basis, as her clumsiness that day had made clear. Finally, after a long stream of customers, the lobby was quiet. She took advantage of the time to tidy up behind the counter before the next influx of hungry people appeared.

"How'd everything go?" Maggie said, coming up behind her. "Did Anna come in yet?"

Angel stopped wiping down the exterior of the bakery case and shook her head. "Not yet." She smiled at her boss. "Things went well. The mad rush just ended and I thought I'd shine this up. Lots of little kids pressing their noses against it."

"Thanks. I appreciate how hard you work here." Maggie regarded her. "Do you think you'd want to meet my friends and me for drinks tonight at Off the Vine?"

Angel dabbed at a nonexistent smudge on the glass. "I don't know. I've got a lot to do."

Maggie frowned at her and put her hands on her hips. "Hey, don't fib to me. I'm a mom, remember? I can tell when someone is avoiding doing something."

Angel squirmed. Maggie and her friends were nice, but they seemed tight-knit and she didn't want to force her way into the circle of friends.

As if reading her mind, Maggie said, "Don't worry. They loved you last time. We're always happy to add new people to our group." She smiled. "Pretty soon we'll have a group that resembles the Ladies of Candle Beach—only forty years younger."

Angel put the rag in a bucket behind the counter and gave her a small smile. "I guess I can make it." Maggie seemed sincere and it would do her good to get out of the house and away from the memories of her mother that kept replaying through her mind when she was alone.

"Good," Maggie said. "It's settled." She examined the baked goods. "You sold a lot while I was gone. Your baking has been popular. We may need to up our daily quantities in the future. For now, can you get started on the pies for dinner?"

"Sure." Angel pushed open the swinging door and disappeared into the kitchen. Baking in her corner of the kitchen was a solitary task, giving her a lot of time to think. She had enjoyed hanging out with Maggie and her friends last time at the local wine bar and she'd been working hard. She deserved a break. And it wasn't like her social calendar was full. Still, Maggie's easy friendship took some getting used to.

In the past, she'd always been busy with school and then work, not allowing herself much time for fun. That was something she intended to change here in Candle Beach. A fresh start was exactly what she needed. Plus, she realized she'd forgotten to ask Maggie about where to go to research the house on Elm Street, so she'd have a chance to do so that evening.

4

"*A*ngel!" Gretchen said as she approached the booth at the wine bar that evening. "We're so glad you could make it." She nudged her friend Charlotte to scoot over in the corner booth. Maggie wasn't there yet, but Dahlia sat across from them, sipping on a margarita.

"I'm glad I came too," she said brightly. She may have been acting more enthusiastic than she felt, but she knew she'd made the right choice. As she slid in to the wooden bench next to Gretchen, their warm smiles made her feel welcome. The happy chatter and laughter of other patrons drifted over the top of the booth.

"Where's Maggie?" she asked as she grabbed a menu off the table.

"Oh, there was something at Alex's school she had to go to first," Dahlia said. "Jake is going to babysit him tonight though so she can come hang out with us."

"Good, she looks stressed. I think she could use a night out." Angel spoke without thinking, and then stared at each of them, wide-eyed. "I shouldn't have said that."

27

"Oh, stop worrying," Charlotte said. "You're right. Maggie looks super stressed. I saw her earlier today and I swear she looked like she was going to snap in two."

"Is she spending too much time at the Sorensen Farm?" Gretchen asked.

The waitress came around and took drink and food orders from everyone.

"I think so. She said Jake was organizing a work party for next week. I get the feeling there's still a lot of work to do out there before it will be in any shape to host events." Angel craned her neck around to make sure Maggie wasn't behind her. Maggie was becoming a friend, but she was still her boss. She didn't want to be gossiping about her behind her back. Luckily for her, Maggie was just entering the wine bar.

"I heard, Sorensen Farm." Maggie put her hand on Angel's shoulder. "Are you girls talking about me?"

Angel blushed and Maggie laughed as she slid in next to Dahlia.

"We were saying how hard you've been working there. When is it going to be ready?" Charlotte asked.

Maggie held her fingers up in the air and crossed them. "I'm hoping for the Sweethearts' Dance."

Charlotte's eyes lit up. "Oh, the Sweethearts' Dance. So romantic. The barn will look lovely for that."

"That's what Jake and I are hoping. It should be a good springboard for new business. Well, it will be if we can get it ready in time." Maggie opened her menu and ran her finger down the appetizer listings, giving her order to the waitress who had returned to check on the new arrival.

"Actually, about that," Angel said. "I forgot to check with you after my shift. When is Jake scheduling that work party out at the farm? I'd love to help."

"Me too," Charlotte chimed in. "I'm not great at hard manual labor, but I'm happy to help as much as I can.

Dahlia and Gretchen nodded as well.

Maggie looked at each of her friends in turn. When she spoke, tears glistened in her eyes. "Thank you. I really appreciate your help. I'll have Jake call all of you."

"Garrett and I plan to go to the dance. It'll be fun, and I can't wait to see the barn all done up." Dahlia smiled at her.

"Does Garrett have any single male friends that might want to go to the dance with a really fun girl?" Charlotte asked, a mischievous expression on her face.

"I don't know, do you know a really fun girl?" Dahlia asked.

Charlotte shot her a mock glare and Dahlia laughed.

"I'll ask." Dahlia turned to Angel. "What about you? Are you going?"

Angel scrunched up her face. "I don't have anyone to go with." Maggie opened her mouth as if to speak, but Angel cut her off. "But I'll think about it, okay?"

Unbidden thoughts of the cherry Danish man flitted into her head. He'd been kind and funny, and wasn't hard on the eyes. Maybe he'd be a possibility for a date to the dance. But she was being silly—he could be married for all she knew. Besides, she didn't need the stress of being in a new relationship. It was hard enough keeping her emotions in check when she was so close to finding out about her mother's family.

"Maybe Garrett can find someone for you too," Charlotte teased.

Angel narrowed her eyes and Charlotte chortled.

Just in the nick of time, the waitress arrived with their food, halting their talk of dates for the dance.

"I'd give anything for a tropical vacation right now,"

Charlotte said as she dug into a cheeseburger. "Beaches and warm sunshine. That's what I need."

Angel nodded. "This is my first winter living where it gets below fifty on a regular basis." She ate a bite of her Cobb salad and then sipped her blended lime margarita, enjoying the fruity scent that always reminded her of the summer parties her mother and stepfather used to throw on their deck.

"Really?" Gretchen stopped eating the French onion soup she'd ordered and put down her spoon. "Where are you from? I can't believe I've know you for over a month and I've never asked you where you came from before you moved here."

"Southern California, near Los Angeles." She shivered. "It was neat to have that snow in December, but I think I'm done with winter already. At this rate, I'm going to have to get a whole new wardrobe." She hadn't realized until now how little of her personal life she'd shared with her landlord, much less the rest of her new friends.

"I'm so jealous," Charlotte said. "I've always wanted to live down there. But the Washington Coast is home and I can't stay away too long. I got a little stir crazy when I went to college in Boston."

"Yeah, me too," Dahlia piped up. "What made you want to move up here? I don't think you've ever told us."

"Oh, just a change of scenery." Her heart beat faster. Should she tell them the truth? Maybe they could help her find her family. Why was she keeping it such a secret anyway? Was this another way of distancing herself from finding out if she had any family left in Candle Beach?

Maggie's eyes met hers. "Did you know someone here? We're kind of off the beaten path for someone to just come to out of the blue." She paused, and then said hurriedly, "Although I'm really glad you did."

Someone near the kitchen must have dropped a serving tray, because the sound of breaking glass caused everyone in the restaurant to stop what they were doing and stare in that direction. Angel could have used that moment of distraction to change the subject, but she decided to take a chance and tell them the reason she was in town.

She took a big breath. "Okay, fine. I'm actually here because my mom's family is from Candle Beach. I think I was born here, although we must have moved when I was about three or four."

"Really?" Gretchen's eyes lit up. "Who is your mother?"

"She died last year and I don't know her maiden name. All I have is this." She pulled the photo out of her wallet, taking care not to crumple it, and handed it to Gretchen.

"This looks like it was taken in the nineteen-eighties," Gretchen said as she scanned it.

Maggie reached for the photo and Gretchen released it. "It does look like the eighties. Look at the poofy hair on the two girls. I can't even imagine how much hairspray it must have taken to get it to puff out like that." She looked at Angel. "Which one is your mother?"

"The older girl. I assume those are her parents and maybe a sister?" She stared at the photo, anxiety welling in the pit of her stomach. What if she had an aunt? Or cousins? "My mom never talked about her family much. All I know is there was some sort of falling out when I was a little kid."

"Is your father from Candle Beach as well?" Gretchen asked.

"I don't know. That's another thing my mother kept quiet about. He could be the prince of Norway for all I know." Angel grinned at the thought of secretly being royalty. Now that would be a surprise. But she'd be happy if her father turned out to be the local handyman. At least she'd know she had a family.

Charlotte held her hand out for the picture. "Hey, I recognize this house. I go running by it sometimes. Over on Elm Street."

Excitement rose in Angel's chest. If it was the same one she'd identified, there would be something to go on. She was almost afraid to confirm it. "The yellow house?"

Charlotte nodded. "Yeah. It looks a little different now, but I'm pretty sure it's the same house."

"I drove through all the older neighborhoods, and I thought it looked the same." She took the photo back from them and stared at the family in it—her family. "But how do I find out who lives there now? Or who lived there back then?"

"You could start at the county offices, but they're closed until Monday. That would be the best bet. But until then, maybe you should check with Adam down at the newspaper office. He seems to know everything going on in this town," Charlotte said.

"Yeah, and Adam's usually in on Saturdays, at least after ten. He'll be happy to help," Gretchen added.

"Adam," she repeated. "Thanks. I'll do that." A sense of relief passed through her. She had a plan now. Check in with Adam at the newspaper and then if that didn't work out, she could research the address at the county offices after work on Monday. She ran her finger reverently over the edge of the Polaroid photo, straightening a slight bend in the plastic-y border.

"This is so exciting. I can't believe you don't know anything about your family. I hope you find them." Maggie's eyes gleamed. "Let us know if there's anything we can do to help, okay?"

"I will. Thank you, guys."

They all smiled at her and for the first time she felt like she belonged in Candle Beach. She hadn't made up her mind whether or not she'd stay in town after she found out about her family, but at least she had friends now.

5

_____

*A*ngel woke up Saturday morning full of hope that it would be the day she'd finally find out about her mother's family. It was only eight o'clock and her new friends had told her that the newspaper office wouldn't be open until at least ten, so she dressed in Lycra pants, a sweatshirt over a tank top, and running shoes.

Stretching her legs on the main street outside Gretchen's house, she peered through the trees at the ocean below. From here, only a sliver of the beach was visible, but something about just knowing the wide-open expanse was there exhilarated her. She took off down the hill at a slow jog, keeping pace until she reached the beach overlook.

When she got to the beach, she picked her way down to the hard-packed sand and ran down the beach, pushing herself to run further and faster. The beach was practically empty, which she relished. In California, the beaches were often standing room only. However, back home, she was more likely to see people wearing swimsuits than parkas. When she reached a creek that was too wide and deep to cross without getting wet, she turned back toward town. To cool down, she walked up the hill toward her apartment, brushing back the sweat that pooled on her forehead and cooled in the chilled air.

On the hike back, she passed by streets lined with charming houses from the 1900s, dating back to the time the town was founded. Had her family been among the original settlers, or had they moved to Candle Beach later? There was so much she didn't know about them—so much her mother hadn't shared with her.

In her apartment, she took a quick shower and dried her hair. It was after nine and her skin itched with the desire to head into town. She was so close to finding out about where her mother came from.

At a quarter to ten, she walked down the hill to the office of the *Candle Beach Weekly*. When she pushed on the door, it didn't budge. *Well, that's that.* Should she wait, or come back later? Would Adam even show up on a Saturday? Gretchen had said he was usually there, but with her luck, today would be the exception.

She opted to take a brisk walk around the block, hoping that the extra exercise would help quell some of her anxiety. In the park across the street, a man was playing Frisbee with his golden retriever, and she watched as the dog raced across the green grass and jumped in the air to catch the flying yellow disc. Then the man turned toward her, and she recognized him as the cherry Danish guy.

Flustered, she ducked behind a lamp post and hoped he hadn't seen her. Although he hadn't seemed mad at her, she'd relived the moment in her mind so many times at this point that her feelings of embarrassment had reached an exaggerated level. To regain her composure, she walked for a few more blocks and returned to the newspaper office.

When she came back, the lights were on and someone was moving around inside the building.

With a deep breath, she pushed on the door. This time, it opened. She stepped into the office and looked around. There were only two desks in the room. One was covered with a random assortment of office supplies and newspapers and the other held a computer and neat stacks of files. Newspaper clippings and framed photographs covered the far wall. A golden retriever ran toward her, nudging her leg with its wet nose. She leaned down to pet it, and then had a sinking feeling that she recognized the dog.

"Sorry about that," called a familiar male voice from the back room. "Otis gets a little excited by visitors."

The man came into the main office, stopping when he saw her.

"It's you," they both said in unison, then laughed.

"Are you Adam?" she asked the man from the café whose breakfast she'd ruined.

"I am. And you're Angel, right?"

She nodded, her heart beating a little faster. He'd remembered her name.

"Did you come here to drop my donuts on the floor too?" He nodded to a brown cardboard box resting on the edge of his desk.

She stared at him in horror. "No...I'm so sorry about that," she stuttered.

Had she completely misjudged him? Was he mad at her about the cherry Danish incident? He'd seemed so nice about it at the café.

His eyes widened and he came closer to her, his hands held limply at his sides. "I was kidding. I'm sorry." He sighed. "I have a tendency to joke about things at inappropriate times. I know it was an accident and I shouldn't have mentioned it."

Angel took a deep breath. "It's okay. I do feel horrible about it though. I know how much you wanted that pastry." Judging by the half-full donut box on his desk, he took his breakfast sweets seriously. The Danish she'd saved for him at the café had disappeared, so she'd assumed he'd come by for it, but she still felt like she owed him for ruining his morning. "Did you get the Danish I left for you? I feel really bad about dropping yours. I'll bring you a dozen next time I make them, okay?" The words tumbled from her mouth in a messy stream of consciousness.

"I did get it. But don't even worry about dropping the other one." He smiled gently at her. "I could probably stand to eat a few less Danishes." He patted his perfectly flat stomach.

She was willing to bet by his lean physique and enthusiastic personality that he was one of those people who subsisted on an overabundance of nervous energy and never gained weight.

"So what can I do for you?" he asked. "Did you come here to sign up for a newspaper subscription? We're running a special for newcomers to town."

She shook her head. "I'm researching something and some friends told me you might be able to help."

His face lit up. "Even better. What is it?"

"I have this photo and I don't know who the people are in it. I was hoping you could help me find out."

He gave her a funny look. "Okay," he said slowly.

She handed him the Polaroid picture. He stared at it for a minute. "Is this in Candle Beach?"

"Yes. I think it's a house over on Elm Street."

He took a closer look. "It does look familiar. Do you know the address?"

She took a deep breath. "Yes, 511 Elm."

"And you don't know who any of these people are?"

"One of them is my mother, Erin." She pointed at the older girl. "The others I'm not sure about, but I'm assuming that's her sister and parents."

"Were they visiting town?"

"No. I don't think so. I believe my mother grew up here, but she moved away with me to Southern California when I was about three years old. I only have vague memories of a house here, but I'm not even positive that it's the same house as in the photo."

"Okay." He rubbed his chin. "So the first thing we should do is to find out who lives in that house now. Maybe they still live there. Can you get more information from your mother?"

"No. She died a few months ago and I never knew her maiden name."

He blinked. "I'm sorry for your loss."

"Thank you. Anyway, she never talked about her life here. I think there was some bad blood between her and her family."

"Are you sure you want to find out who they are?" Adam's warm eyes met hers.

She took a deep breath. Was she sure? "No, but I need to know if I have family. I was an only child and my mother and stepfather are both gone now. It's time to find out."

He gave her an appraising look. "Okay then. Let's get started." He sat down at his computer and tapped in the address information. He scanned the screen. "Looks like that house has been owned by the Montgomery family for the last two years. The county website doesn't list the prior owners. They're working on updating their computerized records to include previous sales, but it will probably be a few more years before that feature is available."

"So the current owners are not the family that lived there when I was born." She slumped in her chair. "And I'm back at square one."

"Not necessarily. If you'd like, I could talk to the family who lives there now and find out if they know who used to own the property."

She stared at him, tears forming in her eyes. "You'd do that for me?"

He smiled at her, his warm green eyes seeming to reach into the depths of her soul. "Of course. It's a long shot, but there's nothing I like better than an investigation and we don't get many of those here in Candle Beach."

She laughed. "I would guess not." Then she sobered. "But thank you. I really appreciate it." She picked up her purse. "I'll check with you on Monday afternoon, okay? Or if you have something before that, you know where to find me. I'm at the café all day tomorrow and Monday."

He held up his hand to stop her. "Wait. I thought about something else we can try."

She set her purse down on his desk. "What?"

"Well, we don't know anything else about your mother, but we know when you were born, right? And presumably you were born here in Candle Beach or in the hospital in Haven Shores."

"Right." Her throat tightened. "Are birth records available online?"

"No." His eyes danced.

"Oh. How does that help then?"

"Remember, you happen to be standing in the office of

the finest newspaper in Candle Beach. If your birth was announced anywhere, it would be in that week's paper."

"Do you have those records online?"

"Nope." He beckoned to her. "Follow me."

She followed him past his desk to an unmarked door in the back of the room. Through another door, she could see a large table and a few file cabinets.

He opened the unmarked door and flipped on a light, revealing rows of shelving stacked with what must have been a hundred years of the *Candle Beach Weekly*. The yellowed newspapers emitted a musty odor.

Angel's eyes widened. "Wow." She walked over to a stack of papers and ran her finger over the date on the top. February 12, 1964. "You must have the entire history of Candle Beach cataloged here."

"Pretty much." He smiled. "That's one of the reasons I love journalism—the ability to capture a moment in time and then reference it on a future date." He walked over to a shelf on the back wall. "What month and year were you born?"

She told him and he checked the stacks until he found the correct year. He pulled a couple of newspapers off the shelf and held them in the air.

"Let's go see what we've got."

He led her out of the back room, shutting the door behind them.

They sat back down at his desk and he handed her one paper and opened another one. "What was your birth date?"

"August 18th."

The newspaper crackled as she flipped through it until she found the announcements section. Was she finally going to find out her parents' full names? Her mother had never even mentioned her father before.

Her heart sank further and further as she read down the list, not finding her name or birth date.

"Any luck?" Adam asked.

"No, you?"

"Not in this one. But we've still got two more to look at. Sometimes the families are so caught up in the birth of the child that they don't get it in the paper for several weeks." He set his paper down on the desk and they each picked up another.

Out of the corner of her eye, she saw him fold that paper back up.

The paper she held was the last chance to find a notice about her birth. Her pulse quickened. Was that her name she saw? Yes, Angel Marie. Born to Erin Thomason.

"I found it. My mother's last name was Thomason." She rolled it around on her tongue. Thomason.

"Let me see."

She handed him the paper and he checked the notice.

"There's no father listed, but at least we know your mother's name now. That should help."

"Yeah, that fits. She never mentioned him. My stepfather was the only father I ever knew." She leaned her elbows on the table and rested her head in her hands, staring at the paper he held. "Now what?"

"Now we figure out where your mother lived when you were born. If the Thomason family was the prior owner, we know we've got a match."

She was almost afraid to hope. "And I'll be able to find that in the county records?"

"Yes. The records clerk will help you. They're open from nine to five on Monday."

"Oh. I can't get there in time. I have to work during those

hours." Her heart sank. She was scheduled to work all day on Monday and Tuesday.

He pressed his lips together, with a look of sympathy on his face. "I'm sorry, I'd love to be able to help, but I'm working on a big story. I don't think I could get down there until midweek either."

She stood. "No problem. I appreciate all your help."

"Glad to help." He cleared his throat. "Maybe I'll see you next time I stop in at the Bluebonnet Café."

"Maybe." Her pulse quickened. He sounded interested in her, but he might just have been making polite conversation. "Thanks again."

He gave her a wave and then went back to typing on his computer. She let herself out, feeling both dejected and excited in the same moment. She was so close to learning about her family, but she'd have to wait a few more days. But then again, what were a few more days when it had already been close to a lifetime since she'd last seen them?

6

———

*A*dam sat at the dinner table on Sunday night, lost in thought. Around him, his family chattered, but he didn't pay any attention to what they were saying.

Maybe if he sold more ad space, he could afford a website for the *Candle Beach Weekly*. Or maybe another bank would give him a loan. That seemed unlikely though, as he'd been turned down for a loan in his home town where everyone knew him. A large national bank wouldn't take a chance on him. He took a bite of ham off his fork, chewing slowly as he considered his options.

"Adam?" A worried female voice cut through his thoughts.

Adam looked up from his plate to see his mother staring across the table at him with a concerned expression on her face. Had she said something to him?

"I asked you if the potatoes were okay." She furrowed her brows. "You looked like you were a million miles away."

He cleared his throat. "Yes, they're delicious." He scooped up another forkful and put them into his mouth, smiling for her benefit. Like always, the mashed potatoes were velvety smooth and perfectly seasoned. Unfortunately, today, he'd been so lost in thought that he hadn't tasted any of it.

Her face softened. "Okay, I was worried, because it didn't seem like you were enjoying them very much."

"Mom, he's fine. Leave him alone," his sister Sarah said from the far end of the long wooden dining table.

He smiled gratefully at her and whispered, "Thanks."

"Well, it's just that he's been so quiet lately. It's not like him." He felt his mother's eyes scanning his face.

"Grandma, can I have some more ham please?" asked his nine-year-old nephew Charlie.

Adam's mother smiled and nodded at her oldest grandchild. "Of course, honey."

He came over to his parent's house every week for the Rigg family Sunday dinner. When his sister Sarah came back to Candle Beach after teaching in Seattle for a few years, they'd made it a family tradition. His sister Jenny, her two kids—Charlie and Kara, and her husband Rick joined them as well. His mother was overjoyed to extend her table and have her children return home every week, if only for a few hours. And, as an added benefit, he got to enjoy a proper meal once a week, instead of his usual diet of TV dinners and takeout. He reached for the tongs in the Caesar salad.

Jenny turned to him, her eyes twinkling. "You look like you have something on your mind, Adam. What's going on?"

His mother turned her sharp gaze on him again. "Have you met a new girl?" she asked, excitement evident in her voice.

He sighed. Of course that was the first thing she thought

of. She wouldn't rest until he'd given her more grand-children.

"No, Mom." He hesitated, his mind flashing back to Angel in the newspaper office with him. There had been something enchanting about the way she studied each page of the archived papers so carefully, eager for any mention of her family. There had been an instant connection between them—more than just a physical reaction. But he couldn't tell his mother about her, because she'd be devastated when it didn't work out. Besides, he didn't really have time in his life for a romantic relationship right now. Making the news-paper a success for the future was his main priority.

He forced a smile. "Sorry if I seem distracted. I've been working hard at the paper. I'm trying to get it online by next year."

"Ah. That's wonderful, son." His father beamed at him before grabbing another slice of ham. "We're so proud of you. Who would have thought that you'd go from paperboy to owning the whole thing now?"

"Actually, I've been meaning to talk to you about that." Sarah grinned at him. "I've been teaching my fourth-graders about journalism and they're all very excited that my brother owns the newspaper here in town. Would it be possible for us to take a field trip to visit you and see where the magic happens?"

He shrugged. "Sure, that's fine. Just let me know when you want to come by. I'll try to make sure I have something exciting going on." He laughed. "You might want to take a trip to the printing press in Haven Shores. That would probably be the most interesting thing for them to see. Not much goes on in my office except for some writing of articles on the computer."

"I'm sure they'll be excited to see an actual newspaper

office. Or at the very least, they'll be thrilled to get out of school for an hour or two. There's nothing quite like a field trip."

Charles nodded his head vigorously. "I loved it when we got to go to the aquarium in Haven Shores."

Jenny smiled. "And remember, honey, you've got the beach walk field trip coming up too."

Charlie beamed. "That will be so cool. Andy said he saw a dead crab last time."

Kara looked up from the pile of peas she was pushing around her plate. "I want to see a dead crab too. When do I get to go on a field trip?" she whined.

Jenny reached over and pulled her close. "You get to go on field trips with me almost every day. Remember, we went to the grocery store yesterday and that nice man let us see where all the food is stored in the back."

Kara pouted. "That's not what I mean. I hate the grocery store. It's boring. It's not fair that Charlie gets to do everything and I don't."

Jenny patted her daughter on the back. "When you're older, you'll get to go on the same field trips."

Next to her, Kara continued to sulk.

Adam's father set down the glass of water he'd been sipping. "How are things going down at the newspaper office? There hasn't been much excitement around town in the last couple of months."

"No, but enough to keep me busy," Adam said. "I'm working on a piece about the logging industry. Also, Ocean-view Estates is finished now and people are starting to move in. I'd like to do a feature on some of our new town residents. Oh, and Maggie Price is going to open the new Sorensen Farm event center next month, just in time for the Sweethearts' Dance on Valentine's Day."

He turned to his sister Sarah. It was time to get the spotlight off of him. "Are you planning on going to the Sweethearts' Dance? Maybe with that teacher you couldn't stop talking about last Sunday?"

She blushed. "I don't think so. It turns out he has a girlfriend in Tacoma."

Jenny frowned. "I'm sorry, Sarah. He sounded like a nice guy. I wish you could be as happy as I am with Rick." She looked lovingly into her husband's eyes and he leaned down to kiss her.

"Eww. Gross," Charlie said under his breath.

Sarah shrugged. "It's okay, I don't really have time to be dating anyway. Teaching keeps me pretty busy."

She turned to their mother. "Hey Mom, how's it going down at the library? How did the latest book sale go?"

Their mom launched into a long explanation about how much money the latest book sale had raised for the Friends of the Library. Sarah and Adam gave collective sighs of relief that their lives were no longer under the microscope.

Adam shoveled mashed potatoes into his mouth as his mother spoke. Charlie and Kara squabbled, kicking each other under the table and causing the table to shake.

"Stop it!" Kara screamed.

"No, you stop it," Charlie grumbled. "I'm trying to eat."

Jenny gave them both the evil eye, and Charlie shoved a spoonful of peas into his mouth, the picture of innocence.

Adam smiled to himself. He loved Jenny's kids, but sometimes he didn't know how she managed to deal with them on a daily basis. He had enough problems developing a relationship with one woman—he couldn't imagine being married to someone and raising two little humans of his own. He cast a glance at Kara, who gave him a cherubic smile.

Okay, she was cute. Maybe he would want kids someday, but it didn't seem like that was in the cards for him. He had his work at the newspaper, and that was all he had time for. If he wanted to make the *Candle Beach Weekly* successful, he needed to put all of his energy into doing that.

An image of Angel came into his head again, but he pushed it away. No, he didn't have time for any type of romantic entanglement. He'd helped her figure out the next step in finding her family, but that was the end of it. Maybe he'd see her at the café again and maybe not. A curious sensation jabbed at his heart at the thought of not seeing her again. He shook his head. He was being ridiculous. He'd only seen her twice. That wasn't enough time for someone to get under his skin.

After dating a girl for four years in college and then having her tell him that she'd never truly been in love with him, he'd come to the conclusion that he wasn't cut out for a long-term relationship. He'd thought maybe his childhood friend Gretchen, the stereotypical girl next door, might be an exception. However, Gretchen had fallen in love with Parker and dashed any such hopes.

No, he was genuinely happy for Jenny and Rick, but he just wasn't cut out for romance. He eyed his mother. She had left the table to carry some dishes into the kitchen and returned with a carrot cake. His mouth watered at the sight of the gooey frosting and the thought of eating the sugary treat. He'd already had donuts for breakfast and a piece of pie after lunch. It may be time to curb his sugar addiction. He stared at the cake again. Nah. As addictions go, sugar wasn't as bad as some.

"I tried out a new recipe for carrot cake. This one has more cream cheese than the one I tried a few months ago. I hope you like it." His mother set it down on the table and sliced into the cake, giving each family member a piece.

He bit into the raisin-studded cake, feeling a little guilty about not telling his mother about Angel, even if it turned out to be nothing. He knew she wanted him to settle down with a nice girl and give her a few more grandchildren to spoil rotten. But she had Jenny's kids, and there was also his sister Sarah to produce grandchildren. Although Sarah wasn't doing a great job of getting married or having kids herself. From what he'd observed, she was more of a lone wolf than him.

He finished his dessert, then wiped his mouth and pushed his chair away from the table. Standing up, he picked up his plate and carried it into the kitchen.

He returned to the dining room and kissed his mother's cheek. "I've got to get home. I'm working on a big story." He needed to make some progress on his research if he wanted to be prepared for his meeting with John Nichols.

"Oh." Her face fell. "I was hoping we could all play a game together. It's been a while since we last played Pictionary."

He hugged her, and then waved at the rest of the family. "Next time, I promise."

She nodded, but he felt her eyes glued to his back as he left.

7

"Angel!" A woman called out while pushing open the swinging door into the kitchen.

Angel looked up from the bread dough she was kneading and eyed her. The woman's gray hair was pulled tightly back from her face in a bun, giving her expression a pinched look—although on second thought, that may not have had anything to do with the bun.

What did Velma want now? Last time she'd been in here, she'd very rudely informed Angel that they were out of chocolate chip cookies and chided her about proper inventory management. The weekend without her had been blissful. The older woman had worked at the café since before Maggie bought it and had earned weekends off through seniority. Now, it was Monday and she was in for another long week with Velma.

"There's someone here for you." She puckered her lips as though she'd just tasted a sour lemon. "I told him you were working but he said he wanted to talk to you about something."

Someone wanted to talk to her about something?

"A customer?"

"Yes. But he said he needed to speak to you."

"Okay…" Angel said slowly. If it had been back in L.A., she would have been concerned about a bill collector, but she'd settled all of her mother's debts before she moved to Candle Beach. She brushed the flour off her hands and wiped the remainder on a dishcloth. She didn't know many men in town. Who could it be?

She tucked a stray lock of hair behind her ear and pushed the door open into the restaurant's lobby, blinking as the sunlight hit her eyes. There were a few patrons in the lobby, but none that she recognized. Maggie was standing at the counter helping a customer, but she caught Angel's eye and nodded toward the entry door.

She cupped her hand over her forehead to see better. A man wearing a polo shirt and khakis stepped forward and gave her a friendly smile. He held a white pastry box in his hands.

"Adam. Hey." She stared at him in confusion. "Did you come here for your daily pastries?"

"I did." He tipped his head toward the box. "But that wasn't why I wanted to talk to you. I have a few errands to run today in Haven Shores and I thought maybe I could help you out by going down to the county office to find out about that house you were researching."

She leaned against the doorframe, unsure of what to think. "Oh."

He furrowed his brow at her. "Is that okay with you? I knew you'd said that you wouldn't be able to make it down there in the next few days and it's no big deal for me to add it on while I'm in Haven Shores."

She wasn't sure what to think. Compared to strangers she met back in Los Angeles, the residents of Candle Beach were amazing. Maggie had taken her in as a pastry chef, even without references, and now Adam was going out of his way to do something nice for her. He may have said that it wasn't a big deal to research the house at the county office, but from her experience at the Department of Motor Vehicles, she had a feeling that any government interaction wouldn't be a quick task. Her intention had never been to stay in town after she found her family, but the town was starting to grow on her.

"Sure," she said hesitantly. Her eyes met his. "That's really nice of you. But I thought you were busy until mid-week."

He flashed her a heart-melting smile. "I finished up early. Don't worry. It's not a problem. I was heading down there anyway and I know how important it is to you to find out about your family."

She nodded. "It is, thank you."

He held up his boxed pastry. "Well, I've got my goodies for today. I'll let you know how things go at the county, okay?"

"Okay." Her heart hammered in her chest. How could she repay him for his help? She didn't have much in terms of money, but she was a good cook. A plan brewed in her brain.

He started to walk toward the door, but paused when she called out, "Wait!" She rushed toward him, coming to a halt about a foot away. He raised an eyebrow. "Yes?"

"I was wondering if you wanted to come over for dinner someday." Her words came out in a jumble and heat climbed up her neck. She peeked at him, not sure if he'd understood her. He appeared to still be processing her question. "I make a mean lasagna."

A wide smile filled his face. "I love lasagna." He narrowed his eyes. "Will there be garlic bread too? Because I can't make it for dinner if there's no garlic bread."

A warmth spread across her body. He was joking with her. "Of course there will be garlic bread. Does tonight work? I'm off at five, so dinner around six-thirty? We can discuss what you find at the county."

"Yes, sounds good. Hopefully I'll have good news for you."

She went back behind the counter and jotted down her address on a piece of paper, then gave it to him. "Here's my address."

"Thanks." He stuffed it in his pocket and then checked his watch. "I'd better get going if I want to catch the county offices open." He waved and pushed the door open, stepping out onto the sidewalk.

Through the large glass windows, she could see him walking away with a spring in his step. A tentative smile and a ribbon of hope that shot through her body surprised her. He really was a good guy. But was this a date? When she'd thought it up in her head, she'd intended it as a means of thanking him for his help. Somehow, it seemed to have turned into a date.

She pivoted and almost ran into Maggie. By now, the lobby was empty, and her friend stood a few feet away with an amused expression on her face.

"I see you met Adam." Her eyes danced. "Was he able to help you in your quest to find your family?"

Angel blushed. "He gave me some good pointers and he's going to do some research for me down at the county offices in Haven Shores."

"Just good pointers?" Maggie grinned. "I heard you asking him over for dinner."

"I did. Just as a thank you," she hurriedly added.

"Of course." Maggie looked like she was fighting to keep a serious expression on her face. "You know, Adam's a great guy." She assessed Angel. "You two would make a nice couple."

Was Maggie playing matchmaker now?

Her face must have been beet red by this point. "I'm not in Candle Beach to meet men. I invited him to dinner to thank him for helping me."

"You may not be here to meet someone new, but that doesn't mean it can't happen. Ask Dahlia, Gretchen, or myself. Love found each of us in the most unexpected way. Once it finds you, it's hard to escape."

"I'll take that under advisement." She looked longingly at the door to the kitchen. "I'd better get back to work."

"Go. But keep what I said in mind."

"I will. Thanks." She pushed open the door to the kitchen and returned to her baking.

Later, making the blackberry cobbler for the dinner crowd, she couldn't help obsessing over her date with Adam that night—if it was a date. She needed to head to the store after work to pick up ingredients for dinner. And her apartment was a mess. She groaned. There wouldn't be much room for error in the timeline if she didn't want him to think she was a slob.

And she didn't want him to think that. She wanted him to like her. It was time she let herself open up to new people and stop being so suspicious of everyone.

~

Adam both was and wasn't looking forward to seeing Angel at dinner. He hadn't been able to get access to the records in the county office because they'd been closed that day due to budget constraints. It wasn't his fault, but still—he'd promised her he would get the information. And he would, but he physically couldn't yet. He wasn't sure how she'd take that news though and he hated to disappoint her.

At the top of the hill, he stopped and stared at the address Angel had written on the slip of paper. This couldn't be the right place. He turned away from the house to look out over the ocean. The water was a dark blue-grey color, hardly a contrast to the gray of the sky and the fog that hung over town. He took a deep breath, and then pivoted around to look at the house.

Yes, his first impression had been correct—it was Gretchen's house. Why had Angel given him the address to Gretchen's house? Were they roommates? He wasn't sure how he felt about that, but he was going to have to find out.

He climbed the steps of the old Craftsman-style house and knocked on the brightly painted blue door. Nobody answered. He knocked again and then heard footsteps coming through the house. The door opened and Gretchen peered at him with a puzzled expression on her face.

"Adam, hi. Did we have plans for today?" Her eyes darted behind him as though she were scanning the street to see if she'd accidentally planned a party and should expect more guests.

He cleared his throat. "No, Angel gave me this address." He looked past Gretchen. "Does she live here?"

Gretchen laughed, a tinkly sound that used to make his heart pound. Now, it just reminded him of the good times they'd had playing together as kids.

"Oh, you're here for Angel. She lives in the carriage house out back."

It was all making sense to him now. When he and Gretchen had gone out on that disastrous date the summer before, she had been renting out her house to earn extra money and living in the carriage house on the property. He'd even picked her up there for the date. He shuffled back a few steps.

"Thanks. I'll go around to the carriage house. Sorry to bother you."

She opened the door wider. "You can go through the house to the backyard if you'd like."

"No, that's okay. I'll just go through the side yard. My shoes are pretty muddy." He lifted one shoe up to show her the mud and grass caked on the bottom. Her eyes widened.

"Yikes." She laughed. "What did you do, walk through a mud puddle?"

"I had to step off into the grass because there was a woman pushing a stroller down the hill and I wanted to make sure she had enough room to pass." He stared ruefully at his shoes. "It was a little soggier than I'd expected."

Gretchen nodded, still hovering in the doorway. She eyed him thoughtfully. "How did you meet Angel? Did she come see you about that family matter?"

Did everyone in town know about Angel's search for her family? He shouldn't be surprised given how small the town was and how fast gossip spread, but it caused a pang in his heart that she'd told other people about it. That was silly though. She had every right to seek out answers from every-one, even if it hurt his pride thinking that he wasn't the first resource she'd turn to as the town newspaperman.

Gretchen seemed to catch his concerned expression.

"Angel's a friend of mine. Maggie introduced her to our little group."

"Ah." He stuck his hands in his jacket pocket, and then pulled the right hand out to jut his thumb in the direction of the carriage house. "Well, I'd better be getting over there."

"Have fun." She grinned at him and then shut the door.

He turned and trotted down the steps, then went through the side garden to the back of the property where the carriage house sat next to an alley. He stared up at it for a moment. *Hopefully this will go better than it did with Gretchen last summer.*

8

At the top of the carriage house stairs, he rapped three times on the door and waited, flashing back to when he'd done the same thing over the summer on his date with Gretchen.

A few seconds later, Angel came to the door with tomato sauce splashed on the apron she wore over her dress. She held a wooden cooking spoon in her hand.

He looked at his watch. "Am I too early?"

"No, no. I'm just running a little behind." She made a face. "Okay, truth is I'm usually running a little behind." She gestured to the couch. "Have a seat; dinner should be ready in about twenty minutes. I'm almost done making the garlic bread. I know that was a deal breaker for you and I wanted to thank you for helping me find my family."

"Sure." He felt even guiltier now that he hadn't had much luck with that yet. He removed his muddy shoes and left them outside. After sitting down on the small loveseat, he sniffed the air. It smelled delicious, a blend of garlic and tomatoey Italian goodness. He felt awkward sitting there alone on the loveseat, so he rose and joined Angel in the small kitchen. She had the oven open and was checking on the lasagna.

"Hey, can you hand me the spatula over there? I need to spread the garlic butter on the French bread," she said as she pushed the lasagna back into the heat.

He scanned the countertop, finally finding a spatula in a blue crock on the counter along the back wall. He plucked it out of the container and swiveled around to hand it to her just as she closed the oven door and turned around, leaving them standing face to face, only a few inches apart. Their eyes locked on each other, and his chest constricted. Her face was flushed with the steam from the oven and a few wisps of hair had escaped the messy bun that she'd piled on the top of her head. She was beautiful. He held the gaze for a moment, then handed her the spatula, breaking the trance.

"Thank you," she stuttered, and quickly widened the gap between them.

"You're welcome." He took a few steps back to allow her room to pass. "Is there anything I can do to help?"

She glanced at one of the few cupboards in the kitchen and then nodded toward it. "You can set the table. The plates and cups are in there and the silverware is in that drawer under the microwave."

"Sure." He nodded. After setting the small two-person table by the window, he stood near it, shifting his weight from side to side as he weighed his options on what to say next. Should he tell her he hadn't been able to get down to the county offices in time? Or should he wait until dinner? He didn't want to distract her while she was cooking, so he opted to talk about something safe.

"How are you liking our weather here? It must be quite different than you're used to in Southern California."

"Oh, it is." She crinkled up her nose adorably. "I'm not sure I'm used to the constant drizzle of rain here, but I love how different the ocean seems. Although it does have that same haze over it that we get down there."

He nodded. "I went to college back East and I missed our ocean views. After graduation and working at papers there for a few years, I couldn't wait to come back home."

"So you're from around here?" She glanced up from icing a round chocolate cake that had magically appeared on the counter.

"Yes, I grew up in Candle Beach." His mouth watered as she layered gobs of fudge frosting on the top and sides.

She caught his gaze. "It's for dessert. Dinner comes first. From what I've seen, you could use a healthy meal once in a while." She busied herself at the coffee pot, getting it ready to brew while they ate dinner.

He smiled. She sounded exactly like his mother, but not in a bad way. It was nice to have an unrelated woman care about his wellbeing. It had been a long time since he'd had that in his life.

She moved the cake off to the side of the counter and rinsed her hands in the sink. Then she opened the oven and eyed the lasagna pan.

"Okay, dinner's ready."

"I can help you get that out of the oven if you'd like," he offered. She had made enough for an entire family.

She waved her hand in the air. "Oh, I have no problem lifting it. I'm stronger than I look from all the baking I do. Hand mixing dough and moving vats of ingredients around is no joke."

"Ah. I don't mind though. I'm not big on standing around when someone else is working."

"Well, you can get the green beans out of the

microwave." She winked at him. "I cheated and bought a bag of steamable frozen veggies."

"My favorite." He grabbed a set of pot holders and retrieved the green beans, moving in a complicated dance with her as they both brought food over to the small table. It was pleasingly domestic, giving him the unusual feeling of envy for married couples that got to experience this sense of togetherness every night.

After they were both seated, he dug into the food. Angel looked up at him expectantly.

"So? What did you find out?"

"Oh." He set down his fork, glancing out the window, then met her gaze. "I went down to the county offices today, but they were closed due to budget cuts. I couldn't do any research. I'm really sorry."

"Oh." She was quiet for a moment, and then nibbled on a green bean. A tear glistened in one eye.

"They're supposed to be open tomorrow, so I'll go then, okay? I know this is important to you," he said quickly. His scheduled interview with the landowner that he planned to use as the basis for an article was tomorrow afternoon, but he should have time to make it down to Haven Shores in the morning. With a start, he realized that although they hadn't known each other long, he would do anything to keep Angel from being sad.

"Oh, I can't let you do that. I'm sure you have something more important to do. I have Friday off. I'll go then."

"They're only open Tuesday through Thursday this week. It's not a bother, really. Investigating things is what I love to do." He gave her what he hoped was a convincing smile.

She seemed dubious. "Okay, but if something else comes up, don't worry about it."

He nodded and took a bite of lasagna. They ate without speaking for several minutes until the silence became too long for him to handle. He wiped his mouth and said, "How are you liking your job at the Bluebonnet Café?"

Her face lit up. "I love it. Maggie and my co-workers are great. Well, most of them. One of them I could do without."

"Velma?" He couldn't hide a smile.

"Yes," she admitted, redness creeping up past the neckline of her sweater. "I swear she seems to find the negative in anything."

He laughed. "She's an institution at the café, first when it was the Greasy Spoon, and now as the Bluebonnet. Everyone in town cringes when they see her heading over to their table to take their orders."

"Then why doesn't Maggie fire her? I get the impression she's not a Velma fan either."

He shrugged. "Maggie's too nice. Plus, what would Velma do for work then? She's been there forever."

"I guess." She moved a piece of lasagna around on her plate. "So tell me about the *Candle Beach Weekly*. How long have you owned it?"

"A few years." As always, when someone mentioned the newspaper, his chest puffed out a little with pride, but this time it was filled with a sense of dread. If he couldn't modernize the paper, he wouldn't own it much longer.

"What's wrong?" She scanned his face.

He sighed. "Well, newspapers in general aren't doing well as more and more people obtain their news from the Internet. Small town papers aren't quite as bad off, but I still need to make sure we keep up with the times."

"What do you have planned for the paper then?"

He took a deep breath. "I'd like to hire someone to build a comprehensive website. Then our subscribers could have the best of both worlds. News from their corner of the world, and online accessibility."

"So if you have a plan, why do you seem so concerned?"

"What do you mean?" He ate the last bite on his plate and sipped from his water glass.

"Your face wrinkled up when you spoke about it."

He sighed again. He didn't want to weigh her down with his worries about the *Candle Beach Weekly*. She had enough on her mind at the moment with finding her family. However, he couldn't avoid her scrutiny.

"Unfortunately, building a website from scratch takes more money than I can currently afford." He glanced at the chocolate cake waiting for them on the counter. "Do you think we can talk about this over dessert?"

She followed his gaze to the iced cake and laughed. "Sure."

While she pulled plates down from the upper cupboard and opened the drawer under the microwave to get out two forks, he cleared the table of the dirty dinner dishes. She grabbed a large knife from the drawer and held it over the cake.

"I'm assuming you want a big piece," she said.

A broad smile crossed his lips. "And why would you think that?"

"Oh, just a hunch." She smiled as she handed him a slab of cake and a fork. For herself, she cut a piece about half the size.

He bit into the cake. It was moist and the fudgy frosting did not disappoint. He meant to complement her on the cake but before he knew it, he'd already put another piece into his mouth. He swallowed and glanced up at her.

"This is amazing," he said.

"Thanks," she said shyly. "I've loved baking since I was a

little girl helping my mom in the kitchen."

"So you and your mom were close?" Another bite found its way into his mouth.

She took a sip of her coffee, blowing on the top first to cool it a bit. "Yes. My stepfather died when I was young, and then it was just the two of us."

He put the fork down and watched her expression.

"But you don't have to feel bad for me, we did okay with just the two of us. Until there was just me." Her mood seemed to darken and her face paled. "I still can't believe she's gone."

"I can't even imagine how painful it must be to have lost the only family you ever knew."

She nodded, and the tears reappeared in her eyes.

He hurried to change the subject. "You asked about the newspaper earlier."

"Yes, you were about to tell me about the website." The color slowly returned to her face.

"There's not much to tell." He shrugged. "I tried to get a loan from the bank, but I didn't have enough collateral to get the money. Apparently a small town newspaper doesn't seem like a safe prospect to loan more money to. Who would have thought?" He uttered a harsh laugh.

"Are there other sources for money? Maybe another bank?"

"I don't think another bank is likely to give me money for it. I'll have to figure out another way." He brightened. "Actually, I was thinking about adding more advertising space to the newspaper. If I can get more advertisers and get our subscriptions up, I may be able to convince the bank to give me the loan."

"I'm sure you'll think of something." She looked down at the table and then up to him. "Have you thought about catering to the tourists? In some of the beach towns back home, they get businesses to advertise coupons and such to the tourists. Candle Beach seems to subsist on tourist dollars, so maybe if you were able to get more of them to buy the paper, revenues would increase."

He stared at her. She was totally right. Why hadn't he thought about that before? He'd been so focused on getting the locals to subscribe that he hadn't considered the potential impact of additional sales from the tourists.

"Thanks," he said. "That's a really good idea. I'll think about it."

A shy smile swept across her face. She asked him about his work at the newspaper and he rambled on and on about the types of articles he wrote. She listened with rapt attention. After a while, he checked the clock. Where had the time gone? It was almost nine o'clock.

"Didn't you say you had to get up early? I don't want to keep you."

"Oh, it's no problem. I'm used to getting up at the crack of dawn. Those Danishes you like so much don't bake themselves," she quipped.

He feigned a glare at her, causing her to break out into laughter. Her laugh was contagious and he found himself joining her. It felt good to be happy for a while. He could tell that it was good for her as well.

She checked her watch. "You're probably right though. I do need to head to bed soon."

"Of course." He stood, and moved their plates into the sink. Grabbing his coat, he said, "Thank you so much for the wonderful dinner and that delicious cake."

They walked together to the door. He put his coat on and then stood on the landing at the top of the stairs, not wanting the evening to end. Angel leaned against the door frame. She was so beautiful standing there that he did the first thing that came to mind, leaning forward to kiss her gently on the mouth.

She kissed him back, a gentle breeze causing her hair to lightly tickle his cheek. He brushed her hair away from her face with his palm, his fingers grazing her soft skin. She stepped back and he froze. Had he messed this up and moved too fast?

He scanned her face. He couldn't tell what she was thinking. "I'm sorry, I couldn't help it."

"I didn't mind," she said in a breathy voice. She stood on her tiptoes and kissed him. The intoxicating scent of her gardenia perfume wafted through the air and he put his hands around her waist, pulling her close. Their eyes locked and they embraced for another minute until Angel was shivering despite the warmth coming from within her apartment.

"I'd better let you get back inside," he said reluctantly. "I've had a wonderful evening with you."

She gazed into his eyes. "Me too. We'll have to do it again sometime." She shivered again, wrapping her arms across her chest.

Adam didn't want the night to end, but he didn't want her to freeze out there without a coat on. He put his hands on her shoulders and gently turned her toward the inside of her apartment.

She laughed. "Okay, okay. I can take a hint."

As she closed the door, he gave her a little wave and walked down the stairs, whistling as he picked his way through the dirt of the alley to the main street leading down the hill into town. He wasn't sure if she'd meant that she wanted a repeat of dinner or of the kiss. Either one was fine with him.

9

"I really needed a girls' night." Maggie placed her wineglass down on the coffee table in Gretchen's living room.

Gretchen leaned back into the couch and kicked her feet up onto the table, narrowly missing the glass.

"Hey, watch it." Maggie tried to glare, but it quickly turned into a grin.

"Sorry. It's been a long week already." Gretchen took a gulp of her own wine.

"It does seem like things have been busier than usual," Angel said. She was hanging out with the two of them for an impromptu mid-week get-together. Each of them had brought a bottle of wine to share and Gretchen had provided the snacks. She pulled her knees up to her chest and snuggled deeper into the plump pillows of the leather recliner.

"Things always pick up with the tourists toward the end of January. After Christmas they tend to stay home, but once their credit card bills are paid off, they start traveling again."

"Yeah, if you think this is busy, wait until we get into

prime tourist season." Maggie picked up her glass and sipped from it, then set it back down on the table a safe distance away from Gretchen's sock-clad feet.

Angel wasn't entirely sure that she would still be around when prime tourist season hit, but the town was growing on her. Plus, she'd heard all about the upcoming town festivals and how beautiful it was in the summer, so she was curious to see it when it wasn't so cold and dreary out.

"Did you find anything out about your family? I saw Adam was here a couple of nights ago. Has he been helping you out with it?"

"He has been helping me. He was going to find out from the county who the past owners of the house I discovered were but the county offices were closed that day. I believe he was going again yesterday, but he hasn't called me about it. I'm sure he's very busy with the newspaper."

"Not too busy to visit you at the café," Maggie said. "It didn't look like he was there just to pay you a professional visit."

Angel's cheeks burned and she fidgeted in the chair. "There is nothing personal between us. He's helping me to find my family, that's all." But how much of what she said was true? Although she hadn't intended the dinner as a date, but more as a thank you, it had certainly felt like one. She and Adam had enjoyed wonderful conversation—and then there was that kiss. That magical kiss that had left her wanting more. With a start, she realized she'd been daydreaming and forced herself to open her eyes to focus on the other two women. Both of them had their eyes glued to her.

"Where did you just go?" Gretchen asked. "Were you perhaps thinking about your date with Adam?"

Angel looked toward the door.

Maggie waved her hand in the air. "Don't worry, we're not going to say anything to him. We're just happy that you seem to be having a good time."

"Yeah, he's a great guy," Gretchen said. "I've known him since he was a little kid and we were playing together in a sandbox in our diapers."

"Well, that was an interesting image." Angel smirked and they all laughed.

"So is there something there with him?" Maggie idly rubbed her index finger along the rim of her wineglass, making the glass ring.

"I don't know," Angel said. "Maybe. But I don't have much time for dating. Plus, I've had some really bad experiences in the past and I don't want to repeat them here. I want to focus on finding my family and hopefully getting to know them." She sipped her glass of Merlot, savoring the oaky flavor. It wasn't bad for an eight-dollar bottle of wine that she'd found in the bargain rack at the grocery store.

"Okay, okay," Maggie said. "We'll stop teasing you about him."

"Fine." Gretchen grinned. "But did you find anything out about your family? That would be so cool if you were able to meet them."

"I've narrowed the house in the photo down to one in town, but I don't know who the owner was." Angel sighed. "That's why Adam went down to the county. He was going to research who owned the house previously."

"That's great. Soon you'll know who they are." Maggie reached forward to dip a potato chip into the sour cream dip.

"I guess." Her stomach twisted. Now that she was getting so close to knowing who her family was, it was becoming all too real. What if they were horrible people? What if they wanted nothing to do with her? She'd often thought about what it would be like to have a bigger family, but once she knew the truth, the dreams about it would be over.

"I really do appreciate all of Adam's help though. I'm not sure I could've done this without him. Thanks for suggesting I check with him first." Her eyes darted in the direction of the carriage house, remembering the sweet kiss they'd shared at the top of the stairs. "Actually, I'd like to be able to return the favor. He mentioned that he's trying to figure out how to increase newspaper subscriptions, to increase ad revenue. Unfortunately, there isn't much population growth in this town, but there is tourism."

Maggie and Gretchen nodded at her.

"We do have a lot of tourists," Gretchen said.

"So I was thinking that maybe the two of you and I could help him come up with some ideas to sell the newspaper to tourists. I mean, there are probably a lot of businesses in town that would like to advertise directly to the tourists."

"I think that sounds like a great idea," Gretchen said. "You know, I could talk to my parents and see if we could give each nightly rental visitor a copy of the newspaper."

"Do you think they would do that? Is that too much to ask?" Angel asked, excitement zinging through her voice.

"Oh, they love Adam. Like I said, we've been friends forever and so have our families. Plus, having a newspaper is good for the town and they would love to help him out. And, I think it really would provide a valuable benefit to the rental customers."

Maggie snapped her fingers. "I just got a really great idea. What if we bundled the newspaper with a morning pastry? What tourist wouldn't love that?"

Angel nodded enthusiastically. "I love that idea. We could sell them both as to-go picnic boxes at the café and maybe Gretchen's parents will be able to offer them to the nightly rental customers." She looked over at Gretchen for confirmation. Gretchen nodded and smiled back at her.

"I bet the grocery store owner would be willing to carry such a thing as well," Maggie said. "You know, our lunch and dinner picnic boxes have been very popular with tourists, I think this would be a wonderful addition."

"Thank you for helping me brainstorm ideas," Angel said. "It means so much to me to be able to repay some of the kindness that Adam has shown me. I can't afford to pay him anything for his help, but this, I can do."

"So you're sure there's nothing between you and Adam?" Gretchen teased.

Angel felt her face flush all the way to the roots of her hair. She stared over her friends' heads at the large painting of the ocean that hung over the couch. From prior visits, she knew Charlotte had painted it. Somehow, she'd managed to capture the essence of the surf spilling onto the sand and swirling around the seastacks, just like the whirling thoughts in her brain.

"Maybe just a little. At least on my part," she amended. "I don't know how he feels."

"Adam's usually off in his own little world. If he's paying this much attention to you, he's probably interested." Gretchen nodded knowingly.

Maggie seemed to notice how uncomfortable the conversation was making Angel. "Is anyone up for a movie? We could make popcorn with lots of butter and eat until the buttons on our pants pop."

Angel laughed. "Don't you have to get back home to Alex?"

"Yeah, but not for a few hours. He's spending time with Jake. It's good for both of them to get some male bonding time in." She shrugged. "Plus, it's a good excuse to hang out with you two. So, are you in?"

Gretchen looked at Angel and raised an eyebrow. Angel nodded.

"We're in," Gretchen said. "What movie do you want to watch?"

Angel settled back on her chair, watching as the two other women bickered good-naturedly over movie choices. The wine that she'd already consumed had given her a soft buzz and she couldn't help but smile. She'd only been in Candle Beach for a little over a month, and she already had good friends, a potential romance, and possibly family here in town. In that moment, life was good.

10

*a*dam left for Haven Shores thirty minutes late, but he figured he'd still have plenty of time to check in at the county offices and then get back to Candle Beach in time for his meeting with the local landowner.

When he arrived at the county offices, the parking lot outside was full—a good sign. Unlike last time, the office was open. He stood outside the door, pausing a moment before pushing it in. A blast of warm air hit him and he removed his jacket. From prior visits, he knew the records office was down the hall on the first floor.

"Hi." He smiled at the older woman sitting behind the records counter.

"Hello. What are you looking for today?" She smiled up at him pleasantly, her mouth covered with a ruby-red lipstick that matched her blouse.

"I'd like to find out the previous owners of a house in Candle Beach." He leaned on the counter while she plucked a form off a stack on her desk.

She stood to hand it to him. "I need you to complete the first half of this."

"Thanks." He accepted it and grabbed the pen that hung on a chain attached to the counter. He filled out the information Angel had given him and returned it to the woman.

She entered it into the computer with a few taps of her manicured nails.

A printer behind her came to life, spitting out a single sheet of paper. She pushed her glasses up on her nose and scanned the document before handing it to him.

"Here are the owners from the time it was built. That's an old house."

He nodded. "It is. Thanks for your help."

In the hallway, he turned the paper over to read the information. This was it, he was going to find out who Angel's grandparents were. Please don't let them have moved out of town, or worse—be dead.

From Angel's photograph, he'd guess that he was looking for whoever owned the house in the 1980s. Bingo. A Wade and Mary Thomason owned the house from 1970 to 2015. That should be enough information to go on.

When he returned to Candle Beach, he stopped at Agnes Barnes's house. He may know the most about what was going on in town, but Agnes knew more about its residents and their personal lives.

She answered her door even before he had a chance to knock.

"Adam, hello." She eyed him through her wiry spectacles.

"Hello." He shifted from foot to foot on the wide wooden porch. Next to him, a pot of fake flowers provided a burst of color on the otherwise dreary day.

"Well, don't just stand there heating my front porch. Come in." She motioned for him to enter, then closed the door tightly behind him.

The air inside smelled like cinnamon potpourri and every surface was spotless. There were few knickknacks to clutter the space, causing the house to look as unfriendly as its owner. But, for all her prickly exterior, Adam knew Agnes had kindness inside of her.

She gestured to the sofa. "Have a seat." She regarded him shrewdly. "I assume you need information about something."

Heat spread across his face. She was correct. The last time he'd paid a visit to her had been to obtain information as well.

He sat ramrod straight on the edge of the sofa cushion. "I'm hoping you can help me find the family of a friend."

"Who is it that you're looking for?"

"Mary and Wade Thomason. They used to live at 511 Elm Street, here in Candle Beach."

Agnes nodded. "Mary and Wade lived there for a long time. They moved into that house in the late seventies, if I'm not mistaken. Before that, the Winstons lived there."

"Right." He smiled at her. "Do you know Mary and Wade? Do they still live around here?"

"Wade passed a number of years ago, but Mary lives in an apartment off Cedar Street, not too far from her old house. You know that six-plex just down the street from the grocery store?"

Adam nodded.

"Well, she lives in the bottom unit, closest to the corner. She moved soon after her husband died. Probably was too much for her to keep the place up by herself."

He marveled to himself about Agnes's ability to remember the smallest of details about the town's inhabitants. Who else would know exactly where each person in town lived?

She looked around her own house. "I'm able to take care of mine, but even when my husband was alive, I was responsible for most of the household management. Mary's daughter and son-in-law live there now." She peered at him. "Why did you say you wanted to know about Mary Thomason?"

"A relative of hers wants to reconnect with her."

"Erin Thomason?"

His eyes met hers. She knew of Angel's mother. But he didn't want to divulge anything to the most gossipy woman in all of Candle Beach before he knew how Angel wanted to handle the information about her grandmother.

"I can't say." Adam rose from his seat. "I'd better be going. Thank you so much for your help."

She nodded curtly and saw him to the door, closing it behind him without another word.

He got into his car and drove back to the newspaper, passing the address of Mary Thomason's small apartment building on the way. He paused in front of it, eyeing the door. It was only one o'clock. He wasn't due to his interview with the local landowner for another hour. Should he stop and talk to her about her daughter Erin and granddaughter Angel?

Although Angel's family wasn't really any of his business, he couldn't help but feel protective of her. Erin had left her family for a reason, and whatever it had been, there hadn't been any contact between her and her parents for most of Angel's life. What if they didn't want anything to do with Angel? She'd be devastated.

But he'd come this far and he needed to know. He couldn't come back to Angel empty-handed again.

Adam took a deep breath and, using Agnes's description of Mary's apartment location, rapped on the door of a bottom unit in the apartment six-plex. He waited, but nobody came to the door. He knocked again.

"Coming. You better not be a solicitor." He heard footsteps heading toward the door.

A woman in her late sixties with short-cropped brown hair streaked with gray opened the door. "Yes? Can I help you?" She peeked through a six-inch opening between the doorframe and the door.

"Are you Mary Thomason?"

She took a step back, not letting go of her firm grip on the door. "I am." She stared at him.

She was probably starting to wonder why he was there. He held out his hand and gave her what he hoped was a disarming smile. "Hi, I'm Adam Rigg."

"I'm sorry, I don't want any." She began to slowly close the door on him.

"No, wait. I came here to talk to you about your daughter."

She opened the door wider. "Rilla?" Her voice was tinged with fear. "Did something happen to Rilla?"

"Oh, no. I'm sorry, I'm not here about Rilla. I came to talk with you about Erin."

The woman's face blanched and she looked as though she'd seen a ghost. She grasped the edge of the door for stability. "Excuse me? Did you say Erin?"

"Yes. Actually, I'm here in regard to her daughter—your granddaughter, Angel. She's here in Candle Beach and she hopes to make contact with some of her mother's family."

"Oh." A far-off look came into her eyes and she pressed her lips together. She motioned for him to enter. "Please, come in. Would you like some tea? I find it helps me to think. I wasn't expecting anyone today."

"Um, sure." He followed her inside to a small living room and sat down on the couch while she disappeared into the kitchen, presumably to make the tea that she'd mentioned.

A few minutes later, she came back into the living room, holding two cups of tea. "My daughter Rilla bought me a hot water dispenser for Christmas last year, because she knows how much I love my tea. I thought it was frivolous at first, but I must admit it comes in handy." She offered him a teacup, which he took from her, then sat down across from him.

"Mrs. Thomason? I hope this isn't news to you, but Angel is up here because her mother passed away."

She placed her cup of tea down on the coffee table and seemed to shrink into the couch cushions. "I did hear of her passing."

Tears sprang from the corners of her eyes, and she reached for a Kleenex from a box on an end table. "Erin sent me a letter from the hospital when she was very ill," she said, dabbing her eyes. "By the time it reached me, she was gone. I'd had no idea she was so sick." She wrung her hands in her lap. "You have to believe me. If I'd known, I would have come to her." Fresh tears appeared in her eyes. "I still can't believe she's gone."

Adam stared down at his drink. So she had known that Angel's mother had died. Why hadn't she made contact with Angel?

"You're probably wondering why my daughter and I weren't close." She took a deep breath. "Or why I don't have a relationship with my granddaughter."

"Well, yes." He couldn't imagine having a family as

broken as Angel's. Hardly a day went by that he didn't speak with someone in his family.

"Well, Angel's probably told you that she and her mother moved to California when she was quite young. Did she tell you why they moved?"

"No. She doesn't know much about her mother or why they left Candle Beach. It sounded like her mother never really talked about it."

"I'm not surprised. Angel's grandfather, Wade, was a very strict man. Some might say he was controlling." She glanced at a photo of a solemn-looking man that hung on the wall near the door. "When Erin became pregnant with Angel when she was only sixteen, he wasn't happy. When she refused to tell us who the father was, it became even worse. He was extremely religious, and to have a pregnant and unwed daughter in his house was difficult for him. After Angel was born, she and Erin lived with us until she was about three, but by then the rift between my husband and Erin had become too great. She took Angel and left for California. We never saw either of them again."

"Okay." He processed the information. "But after your husband passed, why didn't you make contact with them?"

She hunched over her tea. "I was ashamed. So many years had passed and Angel was a full-grown woman, not the little girl who'd left here." She peered at him. "What would they think of me? I allowed my husband to shun our daughter." She stared at his portrait again. "He wasn't all bad." She looked Adam straight in the eyes and said fiercely, "but I shouldn't have let him keep me from Erin and Angel. I should have been there for them. It's my deepest regret."

"I'm sure they would have understood," he said. "And Angel wants a relationship with you now. You may not be able to regain the years you lost with your daughter, but you have an opportunity to right some of what happened in the past."

She began to actively cry and he stared down at his tea.

"I can't," she said through the tears.

His head shot up. "What do you mean, you can't?"

"I can't meet Angel. She'll hate me for what I've done."

"No, she won't. Angel has grown into a wonderful, kind woman. She'll forgive you." He crossed over to stand next to her, crouching by her chair to look into her eyes. "Look, she doesn't have any other family and is completely alone. She wants to meet you more than anything. Well, she doesn't know I'm here or that you are still here in town, but if she did, she'd be thrilled."

She sobbed and he handed her another Kleenex. After wiping her face, she said, "I can't do it. Please tell her I'm sorry."

"You need to meet her," he said firmly. He knew if she met Angel, she wouldn't regret her decision. "What if I set something up between the two of you?"

She sat up. "No, please don't tell her about me. It's better this way."

He eyed her. "Respectfully, it's not. She'll be crushed that you don't want to meet with her."

She looked out the window at the far side of the living room. "You don't have to tell her about me."

"I do," he said gently. "I can't keep this from her forever. I really think you two should meet. Please. I can help arrange a meeting if you'd like."

"No. I'll contact her myself. But not yet. I need some time to think."

He sat back down on the couch. "How much time?" He didn't know how long he could keep the secret from Angel.

"I don't know."

"Mary, I'm going to need to tell her soon. I'll give you two weeks, but then I'm going to tell her about you and the rest of her family here. She knows I'm looking for her family, and I can't keep it from her for much longer than that."

"Alright. I'll tell her myself." She glanced at a calendar on the wall and took a deep breath. "Two weeks."

He rose from the couch and walked over to her, laying his hand on her shoulder. "You will love her and she will forgive you, I promise."

She nodded. "I hope so," she said tearfully.

"I'll let myself out." He motioned to the door.

She nodded again and he exited the apartment. It wasn't until he was outside that he remembered his appointment with the local landowner. With a sinking feeling, he checked his watch. He'd been with Mary much longer than he'd anticipated and it was now two-thirty, half an hour past the time he was supposed to conduct the interview.

He closed his eyes briefly. There wasn't much of a chance that John Nichols would reschedule, given his busy schedule. Had all that research about the logging industry been for naught? And now he didn't have the big story he needed. He drove back to the newspaper office to call him, but he wasn't holding out much hope for a miracle. If things worked out for Angel and her grandmother, though, it would all be worth it.

11

On her lunch break, Angel rushed out of the Bluebonnet Café's kitchen and jogged down to the *Candle Beach Weekly* offices. She hoped Adam would be there so she could tell him all about the plan she had devised with Maggie and Gretchen. Maybe he'd even have news about her family from his visit down at the county offices.

By the time she reached the newspaper office, her face was flushed and her hair had fallen out of the bun she wore it in for baking. She burst into the office, expecting to see Adam sitting alone at his desk.

"I've got some good news," she called out, before realizing there was another person present.

He said something to the man he was speaking with, and then walked over to her.

"Angel. It's nice to see you. Did we have plans?" He seemed happy she was there, but she could see she was interrupting something important.

"No, no, sorry." Her eyes darted to the man at the desk, who was scrolling through something on his phone. "I had something to tell you, but you're with someone." Shoot. Why was she so impetuous? This was his place of business, not the local bar. She turned to walk away.

He put his hand on her shoulder to steady her and looked at her with his warm blue eyes. "Hey, where are you going? We're almost done here. Why don't you wait over there, okay?" He gestured with his chin to a few chairs lined up by the front windows.

She took a deep breath and nodded, then sat down. She wound her hair back up in a bun and stared around the office. After a few minutes, she checked her watch anxiously. She'd need to leave in another ten minutes to make it back to work in time. Her fingers tapped on the wooden chair arm. With the excitement of her proposal to increase Adam's business coursing through her veins, she couldn't sit still. She rose and walked over to view the framed newspaper clippings that hung on the wall. Behind her, she heard the door swing shut.

"Those are from the early 1900s, when Candle Beach was founded." Adam reached over her shoulder to point to the yellowed clippings. Her pulse quickened when his arm touched hers. "The paper has been in existence ever since. Over a hundred years of history in these offices." He stepped back and she turned around to face him. He frowned. "I just hope it doesn't end with me."

Her excitement bubbled up. "It doesn't have to."

He tilted his head to the side. "What do you mean? If I don't get the subscribers and ad revenues to increase, I'll lose this place."

"I told Gretchen and Maggie about how you needed money to fund the new website."

His eyebrows rose. "You did?"

"Yeah, we came up with a plan to save the newspaper." She grinned at him.

He motioned to his desk. "Well, I'd definitely like to hear it. Have a seat." They both sat down.

Her feet bounced up and down as she perched on the edge of the chair. "So you want to increase circulation, right?"

He nodded.

"Well, remember our conversation about selling ads to local merchants to market to the tourists? I think there's a lot you can do with that idea."

Adam sighed and leaned back in his chair. "I've been thinking about approaching businesses about additional advertising, but I'm not sure how I can get the tourists to buy a paper. I feel like I already do everything I can to market to them. There's a sales box right outside the property rental offices and one in front of the café. I can't exactly force them to buy one."

"No, but that doesn't mean you can't get the newspaper to them. Gretchen said we could arrange for every nightly rental client to get a newspaper when they check in. She said her parents are willing to give it a trial run and see how customers respond."

"Hmm. That would help with circulation, but I don't know that it will be enough." He put his hands on the desk and smiled at her. "But thank you. It's a start."

She held the palm of her hand up to him. "Wait, there's more to the plan. What if we bundle the newspaper with a fresh pastry from the café? We could box them up and sell them to customers at the grocery store, the café, give them to the nightly rental customers, maybe even at some of the other local business. Isn't that what every tourist wants—a life of luxury, eating a leisurely breakfast of something decadent while reading the newspaper?"

His eyes narrowed and he nodded slowly. She could tell the wheels were turning in his head. A smile crept across his lips. "That could work. I bet we'd double our circulation."

She beamed at him. "I told you." Then she glanced at her watch. "I've got to get back to work, but we can talk about this later, okay?"

"Yes, definitely. Actually, would you be interested in grabbing a pizza and going bowling tomorrow night?" His eyes shifted to the side until she answered, as if worried about how she'd respond.

Her heart pounded in her chest. A date? She took a deep breath. "I'd like that."

"Then it's a date. How is six o'clock? I can pick you up." He smiled shyly at her.

She nodded. "Sure."

They stared at each other awkwardly for a moment, then he jutted his thumb toward his desk.

"Well, I'd better get back to work."

"Me too." She checked her watch. Her lunch break was over in a few minutes, just long enough to get back to the café.

"I'll see you tomorrow night." She gave him a little wave and then walked out of the newspaper office. She had her answer—he was interested in her—and they even had a date planned now. The whole way back to the café, she was walking on air. It wasn't until she was back at the café that she remembered that she'd planned to ask him if he'd found anything out about her family. It didn't really matter, she'd see him the next evening anyway. Her stomach fluttered at the thought of seeing Adam again.

When she entered the café's kitchen still in a daze, Maggie stopped her.

"Are you okay?" Maggie cocked her head to the side.

"Yes, actually, I just came back from talking to Adam about our idea of bundling the newspaper and a pastry in a box."

"Aha. That explains it." She nodded knowingly, wearing a sly smile.

"Explains what?"

"That goofy grin you have on your face. You looked just like that last night when you were talking about him."

"No," Angel protested. "I'm just excited about this plan. I think it will really help the newspaper. And it will be good marketing for the café as well," she added quickly.

"Uh-huh. The café. Right..." Maggie winked at her. "It has nothing to do with seeing Adam."

"Well, maybe a little bit." Heat swept over her as she remembered the kiss she and Adam had shared when he left her apartment Monday night. It had been good to see him again.

"Okay, okay. Sorry if I'm pressuring you. I've just been so happy with Jake in my life and I want everyone to experience the same happiness." She twisted her engagement ring, smiling dreamily at it.

"I know, but Adam and I just met. I'm not sure things will work out between us. We haven't even been out on a real date yet." She regarded Maggie wistfully. Would that ever be her? Probably not. It seemed like some people were able to get their happily ever afters, but she'd kissed a lot of frogs and none of them had turned into a handsome prince who would whisk her off her feet. Adam seemed nice, but they all did at first.

But that kiss—it had been brief, but had promised much

more. She couldn't help smiling.

"Aha, there's that goofy grin again," Maggie said.

"Okay, okay." She changed the subject. "How are things going at the Sorensen Farm?"

Maggie's expression darkened. "It's going. Not as fast as I'd like."

They moved aside to allow a waitress to pass.

"Will it be ready in two weeks?"

Maggie sighed. "I think so."

"Do you need any help? I told Jake I'd be at the work party next week, but if you need more help, just let me know."

"I think I'll feel better after the work party. I'm probably just spinning on this because it's been so busy here that I haven't been able to devote as much time to the Sorensen Farm project as I'd like. Luckily, Jake has been a big help with it."

"Okay, but don't be afraid to ask for help." She squeezed Maggie's arm. "I think the whole town is looking forward to the dance. I keep hearing chatter about it when I'm at the register."

"I hope so. A lot is riding on it being a success." Maggie took a deep breath. "We've been jabbering over here for a long time. We should probably both get back to work."

Angel returned to work, but visions of dancing with Adam at the Sweethearts' Dance kept popping into her head. Was it too early in their relationship to ask him to a dance like that? They'd only met recently and it sounded like it was a big deal in town. But she rather liked the idea of spending an evening spinning around a dance floor, safe in his arms. She blushed again. Any more thoughts about Adam needed to wait until she was home from work, or her co-workers would start to wonder what was wrong with her.

12

*A*ngel assessed her appearance in the mirror. Was she ready for her date? Adam had told her they'd be going bowling and having pizza, so she didn't want to dress up too much, but still wanted to look nice.

Casual and comfortable clothes, check. Hair and makeup, check. Facial expression...terror. She took a deep breath and then smiled at her reflection. Not quite there yet. She retreated to the couch, pulling her knees up to her chest.

She really liked Adam. She hadn't wanted to, but there was something about him that made her feel at ease with him. Her friends had vouched for him, so why was she still worried and waiting for the other shoe to drop?

Relationships had never come easy to her before. Her last boyfriend had borrowed money from her and skipped town. After that, she'd vowed to be more choosy and hadn't let anyone get close to her—until now.

Knock, knock. He was here.

She sucked in her breath, straightened her cotton blouse and opened the door.

Adam stood on the landing at the top of the stairs with his back to her, gazing out at the ocean. He turned when he saw her and a slow smile slid across his face. "You look nice."

Angel's heart fluttered at his observation. Such a simple thing to say and yet it affected her so greatly. She pushed her arms through her jacket sleeves and he helped her settle it around her shoulders.

"Thank you. I'm excited to be going out tonight."

They walked down the steps single file, and then he reached for her hand as he led her to his bright orange car, opening the passenger door for her. She sat down and smiled to herself as he closed the door behind her.

"Pizza is good with you, right?" He glanced over while driving. "A few weeks ago, I reviewed a pizza place in Haven Shores that's phenomenal."

"I love pizza." She wasn't sure what to say to him. "Do you do many restaurant reviews? I hate to admit it, but I haven't read much of the *Candle Beach Weekly* since I came to town." She quickly added, "But I plan to pick one up this week."

He shrugged. "I don't do a lot, but sometimes I'll review one that someone in town mentions to me. I like to make sure what we have in the paper is relevant to our customers."

"Well, I know the paper is very well respected. I see customers in the café reading it all the time."

He didn't respond and she stared out the window for a minute before turning back to him.

"Hey, did you find anything out about my family? Were the county offices open?" She watched his profile.

His jaw clenched and he tightened his grip on the wheel. "Uh, I have a lead, but I don't have anything definite yet. I'll let you know when I do."

89

"Okay, thank you so much for doing this. I really appreciate it." Why had he visibly tensed when she asked if he'd found anything? Had the visit to the county been that awful?

His shoulders relaxed as he turned into the pizzeria's parking lot. "No problem. I'm excited for the possibility of you meeting your family."

She nodded. "Me too." She must have imagined his reaction to her question about finding out who'd lived in the house on Elm Street.

He opened her door and they walked into the restaurant together, where they were seated right away.

After they placed their pizza order, she asked, "So tell me about you. Do you have a big family? Or are you an only child? Does your family live around here?"

"Whoa." He put his hands up in mock defense and laughed. "Who's the reporter here?"

"Well, you know everything about me and I know very little about you. It's only fair." She sipped her water and gazed up at him.

He answered with a twinkle in his eyes. "I'm the middle child, and the only boy. One older sister, Jenny and one younger sister, Sarah. They both live here in town, as do my parents."

"Do you have any nieces or nephews?"

"I do. One of each—Jenny's kids."

The waitress brought a beer for him and Pepsi for her. She ripped the paper off her straw and stuck it in her drink.

"I'm jealous. I always thought it would be fun to have a big family."

He laughed. "It is nice to have them around. We get together every Sunday for dinner at my parents' place. And I meet my mom for coffee once a week."

"Ah, so you're a mama's boy," she teased.

He reddened. "My ex-girlfriend used to say the same thing."

"So I *was* right."

He glared at her and she laughed. Being with Adam was a heady feeling, a relationship that was full of possibilities.

The pizza came and they dug in, gooey strings of cheese hanging from their slices as they ate.

"This is amazing." Angel took another bite. It may not have been a ladylike food to eat on a date, but it was way too delicious for her to care. It didn't really matter anyway because Adam had already mowed through his first piece of pizza and was halfway through his second. He probably hadn't even noticed when a piece of pepperoni had fallen off the pizza into her lap.

He stuffed the last bite of the slice of pizza he had been eating into his mouth. "You know, I don't really know much about your life back in Los Angeles. Are you planning to stay here permanently? Or do you have friends back there?"

She dabbed at her mouth with a paper napkin and took a swig of Pepsi. "I have friends there, but none are close friends. My mother is gone, so there's really nothing holding me in California. As for moving here on a permanent basis, I don't know."

"Well, I hope you stay." He grinned at her, the dimples in his cheeks giving him a boyish appearance.

His questions gave her pause. She hadn't thought too much about how long she'd stay in Candle Beach. Her main focus had been to find out anything she could about her family and to earn enough money to live on while she did so. Now, her job was more stable and she was so close to finding her family. Maybe that would be a reason to stay. But what if they didn't want anything to do with her?

She glanced up at Adam, who was happily eating another slice of pizza. She shook her head. She was starting to think that he may be a reason she'd like to stick around.

After finishing their dinner, they walked down the street to the bowling alley. She eyed the neon-lit sign and dug her hands into her pockets. The Haven Shores Bowl-O-Rama. Well, there was a first time for everything. They pushed open the door and walked into chaos. Outside, it was quiet, but once inside, she had to get closer to him to be heard.

"How does this work?" She scanned the room. There were ten lanes, with about half of them occupied. People walked by carrying shoes that looked like they were made out of plastic.

"Do we have to wear those?" She pointed at a woman holding the funny shoes.

Adam gave her a quizzical look. "Have you never been bowling?"

She scrunched up her face. "No."

"Seriously?" A broad grin broke out on his face. "This is going to be fun. You'll love it." He pointed at a counter against the back wall. "But yes, you'll have to exchange your shoes for theirs."

They got their shoes and lane assignment and chose bowling balls. Angel stared dubiously at the lane.

"Maybe I need bumpers like those little kids are using." She pointed at a family two lanes over.

"You'll be fine. I'll teach you." He winked at her and warmth spread over her.

So this was what it was like to be with an honest, hard-working guy. It felt pretty good to feel so comfortable around a date.

He demonstrated to her how to move and swing her arm

back. The first ball went in the gutter, but the second made it all the way to the end of the lane.

"I got three pins!" She jumped up and down and hugged him.

He beamed at her and held her close to him a little longer than necessary. "Told you I was a good teacher."

After they finished the game, she sat down on a seat. "I'm so glad I can take these flat shoes off." She rubbed her feet and gave him a shy smile. "But I loved it."

He returned their shoes and brought hers back.

"Thanks." She put them back on and he held out his hand.

"Do you have time for a little stroll? I love walking this stretch of the beach at night. We can drive down there and park at the access trail."

She checked her watch. It was getting late and she had to get up early to work, but she didn't want the date to end yet."Sure."

It was even quieter outside than it had been before. Combined with the crisp evening air and slight breeze off the ocean, every sensation seemed heightened. They drove to the beach parking lot and got out.

Here, the wind was stronger, and though cold, not entirely unpleasant. Still, she shivered.

"Brr." She wrapped her arms around the thin sweater that had been adequate for a short walk between the car and their destination, but out on a Washington beach in the winter, not so much.

"Here." He took off his jacket and wrapped it around her shoulders.

"Oh no, I don't want you to freeze."

"Don't worry about it. I've got a sweatshirt on. I'm fine."

He squeezed her hand and a tingling sensation shot through her body.

They walked along the wet sand near the water, moonlight illuminating their path.

"This is beautiful." She stopped and gazed out at the silvery darkness. Then she felt his eyes on her face. "What?"

He smiled and brushed back a lock of hair that had blown into her eyes. He tilted her chin up, and kissed her lightly. Their eyes met. She tentatively placed her hands on his shoulders. He wrapped his arms around her waist, pulling her close and warming her considerably.

She closed her eyes and deepened the kiss, her hands sliding over his shoulders to rest on his neck. A few other people had been walking on the beach, but now she felt as though she and Adam were alone in their own little world.

Ice cold water splashed over the tops of her tennis shoes, breaking the trance.

"Aah!" she cried out. Adam grabbed her hand and they darted away from the incoming tide, laughing.

Once safe from the waves, he planted a playful kiss on her lips. Her face felt warm, although she didn't know if it was from being close to him or from their quick retreat from the waves. She held her face up, allowing the wind to cool her skin.

Next to her, Adam's watch lit up and she saw him check the time. He turned back to her.

"It's getting late. We'd better get back to Candle Beach."

She nodded. He wrapped his arm around her and they walked back toward the car. She found herself dragging her feet. When the night was over, would the magic between them end too? Almost everyone in her life had disappointed her and although Adam seemed like a great guy, what were the odds that he would he be the one person who came through for her in the end?

He drove her home and walked with her to the foot of the carriage house stairs. She stood on the bottom step.

"Well, thank you for a wonderful evening. I had fun. I'd never have guessed bowling could be so entertaining." She removed his jacket that still hung around her shoulders and handed it to him. "Thanks for this too." She laughed self-consciously. "I suppose if I'm going to stick around, I'll need some more weather-appropriate clothing. My Southern California clothes aren't going to cut it here." A gust of wind whipped past them and she shivered.

Adam stepped closer to her, their bodies almost touching, and then, holding his coat over her back, pulled her close so that they stood there together, not touching, but connecting intimately just the same. She put her hands on his shoulders to keep her balance, enjoying the sensations.

Kissing him was different this time—with the step leveling the difference in their heights, she didn't even have to look up at him. Now, she could stare directly into his sparkling green eyes and get lost in them. She'd forgotten to turn on the carriage house's exterior light, so only the moon illuminated his face. With every breath, she became more entranced. He moved one hand and stroked her face with his thumb, then leaned in and let his lips touch hers. When their lips met, it was like fireworks exploding inside of her. She inched closer to him and wrapped her fingers around the nape of his neck, never wanting the kiss to end.

All too soon, he broke apart from her. He brushed her hair back from her face and looked into her eyes.

She stared at him, slightly confused at the abrupt transition. He smiled back at her gently.

"It's getting late. I want to make sure you get some sleep."

She attempted to process what he'd said. Sleep had been the last thing on her mind and she was pretty sure she was too keyed up to fall asleep any time soon. Still, he was probably right.

"Alright." She sighed. "I did have a lovely time. I'll see you tomorrow?"

"Yes. Maybe we can grab lunch?"

She nodded. "I'd like that." She kissed him quickly on the cheek, and then climbed up the stairs. He waited until she'd unlocked the door to return to his car.

She closed the door on the still night. In the kitchen, she prepared a cup of peppermint tea and sat by herself at the table for two. In the past, the apartment had seemed to be barely big enough for one person, but now she found herself feeling very alone. Having Adam over for dinner had made the apartment feel cheery and now it felt empty.

After finishing her tea, she put the cup in the sink and got ready for bed. She still wasn't tired, but Adam was right. She needed to get some sleep. Flopping down on the bed, she found herself thinking about how perfect the evening had been, and then fell asleep with a smile on her face.

13

"*A*dam." Gretchen gave him a puzzled look. "What's up with you? You keep staring off into space."

"Sorry." He put down the box of newspapers he was carrying and met her gaze. "I'm a little distracted."

She set her box down next to the others in the property management office. Maggie had brought over several dozen blueberry muffins and some white boxes earlier. They planned to tie a newspaper on to the box with a blue ribbon. If this worked out, he hoped to order ribbons emblazoned with the name of the town. For now, they were on a bare bones budget.

"Are you that worried about the newspaper?" She peered into his eyes.

He sighed. "No. Well, yes, but that's not what's bothering me."

Gretchen's family had generously offered the use of the storage room in their property management office to prepare the box and newspaper bundles. They'd thought about doing it at the *Candle Beach Weekly*, but it made more sense to make them where they'd be handed out.

She sat down on one of the metal padded chairs and patted the chair next to her. "Sit."

He obliged, sitting with his knees out and leaning against the rigid chair back.

She turned slightly to see his face. "So what is going on with you?"

He fidgeted in his chair, wrapping his thumbs around each other. "It's nothing." He glanced at the open door. He appreciated Gretchen's help, but he didn't feel like confiding in her. The secret he was keeping from Angel was eating away at him, like a caterpillar slowly making holes in a leaf.

"Adam. I've known you since we were in kindergarten. Something's bothering you."

"I don't really want to talk about it."

"I'm not taking no for an answer. Spill." She shifted her chair to face him directly.

There was no easy way out of the situation for him. He sighed. "Okay. You know how Angel is looking for her family?"

She tilted her head to the side. "Yeah, so? You're helping her out with that, right?"

He held his head in his hands, and then looked up at Gretchen. "Yes. That's the problem."

"It's a problem to be helping her? Or you found something out about her family that she won't want to know?" Her eyes widened. "They don't want anything to do with her, do they?"

"Something like that." He stood, pacing back and forth in the small room. "I did find her grandmother. It turns out that her mother ran away from home when Angel was only a baby because her parents didn't approve of her having a child out of wedlock."

"And they still want nothing to do with her?"

"Well, her grandfather is dead, and her grandmother seems ashamed of how they treated Angel's mother." He ran his fingers through his hair. "When she first asked me to help, I thought that this would be an easy project."

"And now it's turned into somewhat of a mess, huh?" Gretchen was quiet for a moment. "You're going to tell her about her family though, right?"

He felt her eyes on him and his composure crumbled.

"I want to. I feel horrible keeping the secret from her, but I promised her grandmother that I would give her a couple of weeks to tell Angel herself. After this many years, two weeks didn't seem like a lot to ask." He added hurriedly, "I told her that if she doesn't tell Angel within two weeks, I would tell her myself."

"But now you're hiding a secret from Angel." Her gaze burned holes in his skin.

He sat back down on the metal chair. "Yeah, and it's tearing me apart. I hated lying to her when she asked me if I'd found anything out about her family."

"I can see how that would be a problem." She leaned in toward him. "But it's not like you're doing it to hurt her."

"Yeah but I don't think she'll see it that way."

"And she's becoming important to you, isn't she?" Gretchen asked softly.

This wasn't exactly how he'd seen things going when he and Gretchen had arranged to create a trial run of the newspaper bundling program. She knew that he'd had a crush on her since they were kids, and even though those feelings had passed, it still felt awkward to discuss his relationship with another woman with her. However, he needed someone to talk to about it—someone who knew Angel too.

"I think she is." His pulse quickened. How had it happened this fast? He'd only known her for a little over a week, but it felt as though they'd known each other for years. Conversations with Angel were easy. He'd never experienced that with any other woman in the past, including his ill-fated engagement in college. Those relationships had always seemed like so much work, but with Angel, it was effortless.

"You could tell Angel about her family," Gretchen said. "But then you'd be breaking your promise to her grandmother."

"Yes." He slumped in the chair. "I wish I'd never found out who her grandmother was, and never gotten myself into this mess."

"But think of it this way, now Angel will eventually be able to meet her family. Did it seem like her grandmother was interested in talking with her?"

He considered her question. "She did, however she was hesitant about meeting Angel after all of these years. She's not sure how Angel will react."

She patted his hand. "I'm sure you'll figure it out. And Angel will understand. She knows that you're a good man." She smiled at him.

He smiled weakly back at her. "I hope so. Please don't say anything to Angel about this."

"Of course not," she said. "But if her grandmother doesn't tell her soon, I really think you should."

He nodded. He had his doubts that Angel would be quite as forgiving as Gretchen surmised. From what he'd gathered, she'd been let down by many people in her past, and he feared that she'd now see him as just one more in that line.

"Now, we better get moving on this." Gretchen jutted her chin toward the stacks of newspaper and pastry boxes. "The nightly rental customers will start arriving in the next few hours, and I want to have a supply of these ready to give them when they check in to their rental properties. If this goes well—and I think it will—I think I can convince my parents to purchase them for every guest."

He nodded. Putting together the bundles would give him something to do, something that would take his mind off his problems.

"Hand me one of those boxes, will you?" He reached his hand out to Gretchen and she pressed a folded box into his palm.

"I think this is going to work," she said. "Pretty soon you'll be the proud owner of a shiny new website for the newspaper."

"Thanks," he said, with a grateful smile. "I hope so."

～

The Sorensen barn was in worse shape than Angel had expected. She and Dahlia had come together to help Maggie out, but now she wondered if it was even in the realm of possibility for the barn to be done on time.

"I think it's going to take more than just a simple coat of paint to fix up this place," she whispered to Dahlia. She glanced at Maggie, but she was out of earshot.

"Yeah." Dahlia looked at the dilapidated barn structure dubiously. "I know Maggie and Jake love this place, but I don't see how they're going to get it ready in time for the Sweethearts' Dance."

"Oh, it will be ready, if I have anything to say about it." Jake put a hand on each of their shoulders. "That's what we're all here for, right?" In a quiet voice, he said, "I know this place looks rough, but Maggie needs to have it ready in a couple of weeks, so we're going to make that happen."

Angel and Dahlia looked at each other guiltily.

"Of course," Dahlia said.

"Sorry, Jake." Angel felt like she'd been reprimanded by a teacher in grade school. She glanced around and frowned. "Where can we help?"

He pointed at the side of the barn. "Grab a pair of gloves and you can start tearing away the weeds from the outside of the barn." He showed them where the gloves were then took off to help someone else find out what they would be doing.

Dahlia and Angel had been working side by side for over an hour pulling weeds when Angel turned to her and blurted out, "How did you know that Garrett was the right man for you?"

Dahlia's eyes took on a far-off look. "You know, I don't really know. I thought from the start that he was attractive, but there were so many things that got in the way of our relationship. However, I think it was always in the back of my mind from the time that I first met him when I came back to town." She stared at Angel. "Why do you ask? Is there someone in particular that you're thinking of?"

"Maybe. But I've been burned in the past and I'm not sure whether or not I can trust him." She shifted her gaze toward the lake, where volunteers were mowing the lawn that reached all the way to the shores of Bluebonnet Lake. Maggie must be very well loved in town to have convinced this many people to help her with the Sorensen Farm's renovation.

"Who is it?" Dahlia's eyes danced. "Do I know him?"

"Probably. Do you know Adam, the owner of the *Candle Beach Weekly*?"

Dahlia put down the hoe that she'd been using to get at the roots of the weeds and grabbed Angel's arm. "Adam?

Why didn't I hear about this before? How long has this been going on? He's such a nice guy. When I first moved to town, he was a big help getting me into the summer market. Without him, I don't know what I would have done."

Angel pulled away from Dahlia, slightly uncomfortable about her gushing about Adam's virtues. She knew her friends, many of whom had recently met their significant others, including Dahlia who was a newlywed, were happy that she had met someone. But until she knew that her relationship with Adam was for real, she didn't want anyone to get their hopes up.

"We've only known each other for two or so weeks. He's been helping me do some research about my family here in Candle Beach."

"Oh yeah, how is that going?" Dahlia tilted her head to the side, waiting for Angel's answer.

Before Angel could respond, Gretchen broke in. "How's what going?"

"Angel was just about to tell me if she had heard anything about her relatives. Did you know Adam was helping her with the research?"

Gretchen froze for a moment, but quickly recovered. Angel wasn't even sure that she'd seen her hesitate. "Yes, Angel mentioned it to us. If you'd been at our last girls' night, you would've known that," she teased Dahlia.

"Hey, I am a business owner. I can't make it to every single girls' night." She sighed. "We've got inventory going on right now. You know, when I took over the bookstore, I knew it would be a lot of work, but I never expected how lonely it gets. Garrett has been in New York for the last couple of weeks, meeting with his editor and agent, so I've just been rattling around the house by myself when I get home late at night. I've found myself planning vacations just to have something to look forward to."

Angel smiled at Dahlia. "Hey, you know what? Next time I get off work early in the day, I'll stop in at the bookstore and maybe we can grab dinner. Sound good?"

"Hey, me too." Gretchen threw her arms around both of her friends. "Now, let's get to work, or this place isn't going to be ready for the dance."

Gretchen joined Angel in cleaning up the debris surrounding a rosebush that had probably been there for forty years. When they paused for a drink of water, Angel looked around.

"It's gorgeous out here. If Maggie can pull off the renovations, I think she'll have a hit on her hands." She removed her gloves and wiped a bead of sweat off her face. "And imagine living here." She scanned the surroundings. The cheery yellow farmhouse sat at the top of a small rise in the land and beyond it were fields bordered by forests of giant old-growth trees. The lake stretched out below, complete with a picture-perfect rowboat tied up at the dock. "Imagine how much fun Alex will have here."

"It is nice," Gretchen agreed. "I remember how devastated Maggie was when she thought she'd lost the property." She shook her head. "I still can't believe Jake bought it for her."

"Yeah, I can't imagine having someone do something like that for me." A pang of envy hit her heart.

"Adam might surprise you." Gretchen smiled. "I love Parker, but he's not the most romantic guy in the world. I think Adam would be."

"Maybe." She gazed at the serene lake again. Somehow the conversation always came back to Adam. They'd barely met and yet all of her friends seemed to think they were perfect for each other.

"So how are the pastry and newspaper bundles doing with the nightly guests?" Angel asked.

"I think they're going to be a big hit." A smile lit up Gretchen's face. "Adam and I brought them over to the property management office late yesterday morning, and almost every single one of our nightly rental guests was ecstatic to receive them. Maggie told me that sales at the bakery have increased too, because people wanted more than just the one muffin that came in their bundle."

"I know, she told me that." Angel yanked out a weed and threw it into the discard pile behind them. "She had me make several more batches of the blueberry muffins for the pastry case both yesterday and today."

"Do you think we should expand our offerings?" Gretchen asked.

"What do you mean?" Angel unscrewed the top on the bottle of water that Gretchen had given her and gulped from it.

"Well, I was thinking that our customers might want some more variety. What if we had two choices for them every day? I was thinking some cinnamon rolls might be a good bet."

Angel considered that. "I could probably add that onto our usual baking schedule." The additional orders were putting a strain on her normal working hours and she made a mental note to ask Maggie if she could work some overtime. Since Adam didn't seem to be having any luck finding her family, she'd need to start working on it herself as well. Increasing her work hours would make that difficult, but she owed Maggie. Maggie was always there to do things for other people, and now it was her turn to repay the favor.

14

"Working hard or hardly working?" a female voice teased.

Adam looked up at Angel with blurry eyes. His work day had started at six, and here it was three hours later and he hadn't left his desk once. A dry donut and a cold cup of coffee still sat on the corner of the desk, right where he'd set them when he came downstairs that morning. He been staring at the accounting data for the newspaper for far too long and his brain felt like it had been filled with sticky cobwebs.

"Huh?" He shook his head to clear it.

Angel smiled down on him. "Sorry, bad joke."

"No, I'm glad to see you, and not only because you're saving me from obsessing over these financials." He glanced at the clock on the wall. "Time got away from me. Are you ready to help me with these?" He motioned to a stack of newspapers and boxes that were piled against one wall. "I talked to Stan down at the grocery store and he's willing to take an order of twenty to start. It's not much, but he said he'll increase it if they're popular."

"That's great. Maggie gave me two paid hours off from the café to help out with this project. I think she's quite pleased with how much revenue it's bringing in already. Gretchen said that her parents are happy with it too. Several customers have left good reviews mentioning the bundles and it doesn't cost her parents too much."

He came around to the other side of the desk, and gave her a hug and a quick peck on the cheek. "Sorry, I should've done that earlier. It's nice to see you."

They'd had a few impromptu meals together since their bowling date in Haven Shores, but he wanted to do something special for her. He didn't want her to think he was taking her for granted. Unfortunately, there hadn't been much time to plan a date yet.

She cocked her head to the side. "You've got a lot on your mind. How are things going? Are the increased circulation numbers enough to be able to afford a new website?"

He shook his head. "It's too early to tell yet. I have to wait until all of the figures are in at the end of the month to see if it's making a significant difference."

"Oh." Her face crumpled and he felt bad for raining on her parade. She'd been so enthusiastic about her idea.

"I'm sure it's helping though." He motioned to the stack of newspapers. "All of those are papers I wouldn't have sold otherwise."

She brightened and walked over to the pile. "Okay, let's get going then. I want to make sure we get them there early." She handed him a handful of unfolded boxes. "Race you." She wiggled her eyebrows at him. "Loser has to buy lunch next time."

"You're on." He loved her spirit and willingness to help. He was lucky to have her. The memory of his promise to Mary washed over him again like an icy cold wave. He couldn't let Angel find out that he'd known about Mary prior to her grandmother making contact with her. She hadn't asked him recently about his search for her family. Although it made things easier by not having to lie to her, it was worse because he knew she trusted him to tell her when he found something out.

They sat down at the table, folding the white cardboard like maniacs. Angel's fingers flashed as she bent sides up and tucked flaps down to form the small boxes. When no flat boxes remained, Angel had at least twice as many completed in front of her as he had.

"How did you do that?" He stared at her rows of boxes.

She wiggled her fingers in the air. "I have to be quick at work, so my hands are well trained."

She opened the boxes of blueberry muffins and, using tongs, placed one in each of the white boxes. He followed behind her, closing them, then they tied the bundles together with a blue satin ribbon. The tantalizing smell of blueberries and sweet muffin dough hung in the air, making his stomach grumble.

Angel laughed and held out one of the extras to him.

"Thanks," he said sheepishly.

"Yeah, I figured you'd waste away to nothing if I didn't feed you." She laughed again, and then grabbed an armload of boxes to take out to Adam's car. As they placed the bundles in the back seat, she asked, "Have you found anything out yet about my relatives?"

Every muscle in his body froze and the bite of blueberry muffin he'd been chewing gummed up in his mouth. He'd hoped they could get through the morning without this coming up.

"I haven't been successful yet. But I'll keep working on it." Technically, he was telling the truth. He hadn't been successful, as Mary wouldn't let him tell Angel about her existence. But he knew that was a mere technicality. It was still a lie.

"Oh," she said in a small voice. "I didn't think it would be this difficult. Maybe I should just give up on it." Her good mood had vanished.

"I'm sure I'll be able to find them soon." He hated lying to her, hated that she didn't know she had an aunt and grandmother living less than a mile away from where she now stood. All she had ever wanted in life was to have a family that cared for her, and he felt as though he were holding that just out of her reach. Nausea rose up through his stomach into his chest and he gripped the box he was holding even tighter. The sides of the lightweight cardboard box bowed in and he released the tension, pushing on the edges of it to pop the dents out.

"I guess. At least we're making some progress with the newspaper." She examined him closer. "Are you okay? You look a little green."

He nodded. "I'm fine. Just tired from an early morning. Hey, are we still on for Saturday night?" Mary had told him she'd tell Angel that she was her grandmother by Wednesday, so he only had to get through the next few days of not telling Angel about her. But, at this rate, the guilt might just kill him.

"Yes." Her face glowed with happiness. "I'm looking forward to it. Where are we going this time?"

"I thought maybe something a little nicer than pizza and bowling?"

"What, like hamburgers and a movie?" she teased.

"Hey." He frowned. Had his date idea last time really been that cliché? Angel had looked like she had enjoyed learning to bowl.

"I'm joking." She sighed. "Hamburgers and a movie would be fine with me though. Really."

He eyed her. "I was thinking more along the lines of the Seaside Grill here in Candle Beach."

"Ooh, I've heard their food is good." She pushed the last box in on the back seat of Adam's car and shut the door. "When do you want to go?"

"At six?" He held his breath.

"Sure. I'm off at five, so that will give me time to get ready."

With every word she spoke, he felt worse. He eyed his watch. "It's getting pretty late. You probably need to get back to work. I can drop these off around town by myself."

"Are you sure?" She hesitated. "I hate to just leave you with everything. I said I'd help. I'm sure Maggie wouldn't mind letting me stay out a little longer."

"No. I'm fine, really." He forced a smile, even though his stomach was threatening to heave from the guilt.

"Okay then." She stood on her tiptoes and kissed his cheek. "I'll see you tomorrow then?"

"Yes. Six o'clock." He got into the car and turned the key. "See you later." He shut the door, wanting some separation between the two of them. He gripped the cold hard leather wheel and glanced out the window at her. She had her head cocked to the side, assessing him. Did she know? Before he could think about it anymore, he drove away.

~

At lunchtime, Angel stopped in at the property management offices to see how sales of the newspaper bundles were going. Adam had seemed unusually distracted that morning and she hoped an increase in sales would help return him to his usual happy disposition. It hadn't been long since they'd started dating, but she'd enjoyed being around his optimistic outlook about life as it had buoyed her own troubled spirits.

"Hey," she said as she approached Gretchen's desk in the back of the office.

"Hi." Gretchen smiled at her. "Did we have lunch plans?"

"No, but we can grab lunch if you want. After baking blueberry muffins all morning, something savory sounds good to me." She smiled back. "I actually came by to check on the newspaper sales. Adam seemed a little off this morning, at least to me. I'm hoping to have good news for him."

"Oh." Gretchen moved some papers around on her desk. "Uh, I'm sure he's fine. There's just a lot going on in his life with the newspaper and all."

She was hiding something, but Angel wasn't sure what.

Gretchen looked around her desk. "You know, I'm excited about the new real estate firm Parker and I are opening, but I am going to miss this place. It's been such a huge part of my life. I started here right after graduating from college. I can't believe it's been over ten years already."

"It will be a big change." Angel couldn't even imagine staying in a job for three years, much less ten. She'd always sought out the next big opportunity. Short of opening her own bakery, there weren't many options for career advancement in Candle Beach. That was another thing to consider about potentially staying in town.

Gretchen stood and motioned for Angel to follow her. "Let's go check up at the front. I know we've had a few people check in, but most of our guests won't be here until later. We're a three to four hour drive from Seattle, so we're open late to allow people time to get here after work for the weekend."

"Ah. That makes sense." Angel nodded. She learned something new every day about the intricacies of operating a business in a tourist town.

Gretchen's high heels clicked rhythmically on the hardwood floors as she walked. They stopped at a counter in the front of the office. A woman in her early twenties sat at the desk, typing something into the computer while talking on the phone.

"Hi, Rebecca," Gretchen said when the woman got off the phone. "We were wondering how the newspaper bundles were doing today."

Rebecca looked up. "We haven't had many guests check in yet, but they've all taken them. I'd say about 95 percent yesterday accepted the offer and were happy to get them. Actually, I even had a few guests come in this morning to ask where the Bluebonnet Café was so they could get more baked goods. I'd say they're a success."

"Great! Thanks, Rebecca." Gretchen touched Angel's arm as they walked away. "See? I told you."

"I really appreciate this," Angel said. It still amazed her how everyone in Candle Beach pitched in to help each other, whether it be with the newspaper or with the Sorenson Farm project.

"No problem." Gretchen grinned. "Now, onto more important things. Where are we eating lunch? I'm starving!"

Angel laughed. "You choose. I'm still getting my bearings around here."

Gretchen looped her arm through Angel's. "I hoped you'd say that. Teriyaki it is." She tugged on Angel's arm, leading her down the street.

As they were both happily eating their chicken and rice bowls from Tasty Teriyaki, Angel glanced up at Gretchen.

"Um, I've been meaning to ask. Is it okay with you for me to date Adam?"

Gretchen's eyes widened. "Of course. There's never been anything more than friendship between us. Well, on my part at least." She stared at Angel. "Do you think there might be a chance for something serious between you two?"

Angel squirmed. "I don't know. Maybe?" She sighed. "It's hard for me to trust people and open up to them. But Adam seems different..."

"Oh, he is," Gretchen chimed in. "I think he really cares for you. I know he's really broken up to not be able to tell you who your family is."

Angel dropped her fork, which clattered lifelessly to the table. "What do you mean? Did he find out who they are?"

Gretchen's face blanched. "Oh, um. That's not what I meant. I mean he's upset to not be able to find anything out. That's all."

Angel scanned her friend's face, but she was stuffing chicken teriyaki into her mouth. Had Gretchen misspoken, or had she slipped and said something she wasn't supposed to divulge? Angel shook her head. Not everyone was hiding something from her. It was time she learned to trust people in her life.

"Okay." She changed the subject. "How is Maggie's cleanup over at the Sorenson Farm going? Did they finish clearing away the debris from the side of the barn?" When she'd left, they'd only been about halfway through and she'd wondered how it would be ready on time. She bit into a piece of tangy chicken. As much as she loved baking, sometimes the sweet smells of all those baked goods could get to be too much.

The color came back to Gretchen's face. "Yes, there's still a lot of work to do, but they're on track for the dance next

Wednesday." A sly smile crossed her lips. "Parker and I are looking forward to going. Will you and Adam be attending together?"

"I don't know. We haven't really talked about it yet." It seemed funny to think that only a few weeks ago, the idea of attending the Sweethearts' Dance with someone she cared about had been a far-off prospect. In such a short time, Adam had become a big part of her life.

"You should ask him." Gretchen winked at her. "He could use a diversion from worrying about the newspaper." She shook her head. "I'm concerned about him. He's always been so focused on his business. I don't think he ever has any fun."

"I think he's okay." She thought about how fun her inaugural bowling game had been and how comforting it had felt to have Adam's arms around her as he taught her how to roll the ball. Her cheeks warmed with the memory and she lifted her face to meet Gretchen's eyes. "But I'll ask him."

"Good." Gretchen finished her food and picked up her plates to move them to the dirty dishes bin at the side of the restaurant. "I'd better get going. It's Friday, so we'll have a lot of people checking in soon." She smiled at Angel. "And every one of them is going to get a newspaper. I'll make sure." She touched her on the shoulder. "I'll see you later, okay?"

Angel nodded and picked up her own dishes to place in the bin. "Thanks Gretchen."

15

For their date at the Seaside Grill, Angel pulled a dress from her closet that hadn't seen the light of day since well before she'd moved away from Los Angeles. In fact, considering how unlikely it had seemed that she'd need a little black dress for her new life in Candle Beach, she had thought about donating it to the Goodwill. Now, she was glad she hadn't.

She held the simple dress up to her body, watching her reflection in the full-length mirror on the back of the closet door. As she turned slightly from side to side, the gentle folds of the knee-length skirt rippled and swished. It was pretty, but the last time she'd worn this particular dress hadn't been a wonderful occasion. She'd been out on a date with someone she'd been seeing for several months and had been excited when he invited her to go to a fancy restaurant downtown.

However, after they finished their meal, he claimed to have misplaced his wallet and left her with the entire check. If he'd been telling the truth, she wouldn't have minded, but after calling and texting him several times after the date with no response, she realized that she'd been dumped.

But Adam was different. This time she'd wear the pretty dress, and she'd have that fairy-tale romantic date that she'd envisioned when she bought it. She dropped the silky black material over her head and stretched her arms around her back to pull on the zipper. She finished the look with a pair of black nylons and black heels with fanciful straps that wrapped around her ankles like ballet slippers. After a quick application of lip gloss and mascara, she was ready to go. Adam had called earlier to tell her he was working at the newspaper but he'd meet her at the restaurant at six, so she grabbed her coat and walked down the hill to town alone.

When she arrived at the restaurant a minute after six, Adam was already there, waiting outside the entrance. He had his back to her and was bouncing up and down on the balls of his feet, his hands stuck firmly in his pockets. She stifled a grin. He looked like a little kid, overflowing with excitement to go trick-or-treating on Halloween night.

"Adam," she called out.

He whirled around, a smile spreading rapidly across his face when he saw her.

"Sorry for the change of plans. I wanted to come pick you up at your house, but I had to get a few more things finished before dinner and I didn't want us to miss our reservation time."

"Don't worry about it," she said. "It didn't take me long to walk here, and it's a beautiful evening." She shivered. "Beautiful, but cold."

His face took on a look of concern. "Let's get inside then."

He reached for her arm and led her inside. They only had to wait a few minutes for their table. When they arrived at their seats, she removed her coat, revealing her strappy black dress.

Adam's eyes widened. "You look really beautiful tonight." Then his eyes widened even further when he realized he may have stepped in it. "I mean, you always look beautiful, but tonight even more so."

She smiled, and hung her jacket on the back of the chair before sitting down. "I knew what you meant."

"Thanks," he said, the redness fading from his face.

"So, what's good to eat here?" She glanced at the menu.

"I've only been here once before, but I'm partial to seafood wherever I go. I've heard the salmon is excellent."

"Hmm." She scanned the menu, and then flipped it closed. "Seafood sounds good, but I'm craving pasta, so I think I'll compromise and get the shrimp scampi."

The waitress came over and they placed their orders.

Adam had been unusually silent about his quest to help her find her family. She knew he had been busy with his upcoming story about the logging industry, but if he wasn't going to be able to research it for her, she wanted to know. She took a sip of water and then set her glass back on the table, lifting her gaze to meet his. "Have you made any progress down at the county about finding out who my family is?"

He suddenly became very interested in the dessert menu propped up against the sugar bowl on the table.

"Adam?" she prodded. "Did you hear me?"

He sighed. "I heard you."

What was wrong? Why was he acting like this? He'd seemed gung ho about helping her before, so what had changed?

He finally lifted his eyes to meet hers. "I went down to

the county a few days ago, and they were able to provide me with the information I needed."

Excitement bubbled up in her chest. "So you know who they are?"

He averted his gaze. "Yes, I found out who your grandmother is."

"So who is she?" Why would he not have told her if he had found her grandmother several days ago?

"I can't tell you."

"You can't tell me. Why not?" A feeling of dread came over her. "Are my grandparents dead?" she asked in a whisper.

"Your grandfather passed away a few years ago, but your grandmother is alive and well."

"Then why didn't you tell me about her?" She stared at him. "She doesn't want to see me, does she? I came all the way up here to see her and she wants nothing to do with me."

His eyes widened. "No, it's not that. It's that…"

"That she doesn't want to see me." Angel finished.

"No. But I'm just not able to tell you who she is."

She stared at him. She was so close to finding out who her family was, so close to having people who were related to her in her life, and now he wouldn't even tell her who they were.

"You're not able to tell me, or you don't want to tell me?" She removed her napkin from her lap and set it on the table in front of her.

"I want to tell you. You've got to believe me." Adam's face was filled with panic.

"If you wanted to tell me, you would." She picked up her purse and walked briskly out of the restaurant, tears spilling down her face. She thought she'd finally found a decent guy, but Adam was just like the rest of them—not to be trusted.

She walked home, fuming the entire way. It wasn't until she walked in the door of her apartment that she realized she'd forgotten her jacket in the restaurant, but she wasn't going to call Adam to get it back. Right now, she never wanted to see him again.

~

Angel lay in her bed and stared up at the ceiling. Adam had lied to her about her family. But why? Why would he not tell her who they were? Could it really be that bad? Did he think so little of her that he thought she wouldn't be able to handle knowing who her relatives were? She'd trusted him and he'd let her down.

She turned to the side and hugged the blankets close to her. Maybe the whole idea of moving to Candle Beach had been a bad idea. While she'd been upset that her mother had lied to her for her entire life, maybe it had been for the best. If she'd never found that photo, she wouldn't be here, wouldn't be feeling so rotten. Waves of pain washed over her. She'd thought Adam was someone she could trust. If he wasn't, what about her other friends?

This wasn't why she'd come to Candle Beach. Disappointment could have easily been found back in Los Angeles. She could go back to Southern California, but there wasn't really anything tying her to it. Here, Maggie needed her at the café. Her boss had told her many times how happy she was with her work and how fortunate she felt to have Angel there. She'd given Angel a job when she desperately needed it, when she arrived in town without more than a couple of dollars in her checking account. Deserting

Maggie now, when she was in the midst of opening up a new events venue, didn't seem right.

She turned to the other side, ripping off the blankets. In her stocking feet, she padded over to the window. Gretchen's house was dark, but the streetlights lit up the empty street on the other side of it. Beyond that, was the vast expanse of the Pacific Ocean. Candle Beach was beautiful, and she would have liked to stay and give it a chance. But if she had no future with Adam, it might make it too awkward.

She filled the teakettle with water and set it on the stove to heat. As a child, whenever something had been bothering her, her mother had made her tea. They'd sit down at the kitchen table together and work out whatever was the matter. Whatever she'd found out about her mother after she died, she still loved her and missed her very much. She inhaled the strong peppermint aroma from the tea, the familiar scent reminding her even more of her mother. The pain of losing her hit Angel now, as fresh as it had been in the week after her mother's death. Tears streamed down her face and onto the table.

Half a box of Kleenex later, she finished her tea and curled up in bed. This had been the worst day she'd had in a long time. Maybe things would look better in the morning.

❧

The next day, Angel walked into the newspaper office, her face stony. Adam sucked in his breath. That was not the face of forgiveness.

"Hi." She stood in front of him.

"Hi." He walked around his desk and handed her the jacket she'd forgotten on their date.

"Thank you." She took the jacket from him, then backed

up a few steps and folded her arms across her chest, staring down at the ground. His heart leapt into his chest.

She was here to break up with him, he knew it.

"Angel—"

She cut him off. "This isn't working. You know it and I know it."

His shoulders slumped. "No, you have to listen to me."

"What is there to listen to? You told me yourself that you knew something about my family, but you're refusing to tell me about it. And you lied to me by not telling me you'd discovered them in the first place."

"It's not like that. I couldn't tell you."

"Of course not." She shook her head, her hands gesticulating wildly. "Everyone is always keeping secrets from me, trying to protect me. Well, listen to this. I don't need your protection." Her chin jutted out and she glared at him defiantly.

"Angel…" he tried again. "Your grandmother— "

"No, I don't want to hear your excuses." She pivoted and strode out the door without another word.

As the door slammed shut behind her, a pain shot through his chest. What had he done? Was it really worth it to keep Mary's secret if it meant losing Angel? He'd thought he could do it, but now he wasn't so sure. Not that it even mattered now. She'd been so mad at him that he wasn't sure she'd ever talk to him again.

16

Angel had debated whether or not to meet Maggie and their friends at Pete's Pizza for dinner. Her breakup with Adam was fresh, and she wasn't sure she wanted to get into it with the other girls. She found herself lying on the couch in her pajamas, staring at some infomercial on TV. *Get it together, Angel. You've got to get out of the house.*

After a shower and fresh clothes, she didn't feel great, but she felt marginally better. They'd arranged to meet at the pizza place at six o'clock, but she must have walked faster than she realized because she was the first of the group to arrive.

"Would you like to be seated now, or when the rest of your party arrives?" the waitress asked.

She looked around the restaurant. There were a few tables left, and even fewer that would hold the five of them. "If there's a table available now, I'll take it. The rest of my group should be here soon."

The waitress led her to a long booth in the corner of the restaurant and handed her a menu. Angel slid across the vinyl seat and quickly selected a glass of red wine from the menu. After giving the waitress her order, she sat back and scanned the room.

After doing so, she wished she hadn't. Pete's Pizza was full of happy couples out on dates, reminding her too much of her recent date with Adam. It was hard to believe that only a few days ago, she'd thought that they would have a future together.

Charlotte was the first to join her. "You don't look so hot," she said.

"Thanks." Angel self-consciously combed through her hair.

"No, I mean you look exhausted." She examined Angel more closely. "Are you okay?"

"No. I broke up with Adam." Her eyes became blurry with unshed tears.

Charlotte climbed into the same side of the booth as Angel, and gave her a big hug. "Oh, I'm so sorry. I thought things were going well for you two."

"I thought so too. But things weren't exactly as I thought. I don't really want to get into it tonight." Out of the corner of her eye, she saw a woman kiss her date on the cheek, and then watched as he fed her a bite of pizza. If she managed to get through this night without becoming a bawling mess, it would be a miracle.

"Is there anything I can do?" Charlotte peered at her.

"No. I'll be alright. This is probably the best thing for me to do. I was going crazy alone in my house."

The waitress came over with Angel's Merlot and she accepted it gratefully.

"Miss, can I order too please?" Charlotte asked. She gave the waitress her drink order just as Maggie and Gretchen came in the door at the same time. The waitress waited for them to get settled and then left with their drink orders as well.

"Dahlia can't make it tonight. Something about inventory at the bookstore again." Maggie flipped through the pizza menu.

"That's too bad," Angel said.

"Yeah, maybe we should bring her a slice of pizza after we're done." Charlotte said.

Maggie nodded. "I bet she'd love that. Inventorying all those books can't be a fun job."

They ordered a large pepperoni pizza and a medium Thai-flavored pizza topped with peanut sauce and chicken.

Angel felt Maggie's eyes on her.

"Are you sick, Angel? I know you didn't have to work today, but you don't look so good."

"She broke up with Adam," Charlotte said.

Angel stared down at the table, biting her lower lip.

Maggie and Gretchen gave her incredulous looks.

"Oh honey, you broke up with Adam?" Maggie asked, her eyes full of sympathy.

A tear dripped down Angel's face as she nodded yes. Maggie dug in her purse and handed her a tissue.

"Thanks." Angel swiped at her face and did her best to convince herself that the breakup had been for the best.

"What happened?" Gretchen asked.

Angel felt odd telling Gretchen anything about her relationship with Adam, because she knew that they were life-long friends. "We just weren't right for each other. We're too different."

Gretchen narrowed her eyes thoughtfully at Angel, but said nothing. Maggie seemed to notice Angel's distress and clapped her hands to change the subject.

"Well, I have some good news. The Sorensen Farm's

barn passed inspection, so we're good to go on the Sweethearts' Dance."

"That's awesome," Charlotte said. "I can't wait to see it."

Maggie's eyes took on a dreamy look. "Me neither. I have so many plans for it, but this will be the trial run. Fingers crossed it goes well."

Gretchen patted her on the shoulder. "I'm sure it will. And I know we'll all be there to cheer you on, right girls?"

Everyone nodded.

Maggie smiled. "Thanks."

The waitress came by with their food and they were soon engrossed in eating.

"This Thai pizza is surprisingly good," Angel said as she took another bite.

"I don't think it's my style," said Maggie, wrinkling her nose. "I'm sticking with pepperoni."

"Have you tried that new pizza place in Haven Shores?" Gretchen asked. "Adam reviewed it in the paper a few weeks ago and I've been dying to try it out. Maybe we could meet there next time."

"Sure," Charlotte said. "I'm up for it." She grabbed another slice of Thai pizza.

"Adam took me there while we were dating," Angel said in a quiet voice. A sharp pain sliced through her gut at the memory of that perfect date.

The conversation stopped and Gretchen's eyes bugged out. "I'm sorry, Angel, I didn't know."

Angel forced a smile. "Don't worry about it. You should definitely try it. It was great."

"You know, I heard there's a new Thai restaurant in Haven Shores," Charlotte said. "We could try that instead."

"I don't know. I'm not big on cilantro. It tastes so soapy to me." Maggie frowned.

"I'm pretty sure they have dishes without cilantro," Gretchen said dryly.

Angel tuned out the rest of their conversation, still thinking about her date with Adam. From her position at the booth, she had a clear view of the entrance to the restaurant. A man came in, who she instantly recognized as Adam. She stiffened. What was he doing here?

He stood in line, waiting for his turn to order. After examining the menu, he turned and their eyes locked. His face whitened and Angel dropped her gaze downward. In her peripheral vision, she saw him wheel around and dart out the door without ordering. She let out a breath she hadn't known she was holding. Seeing him had been ten times worse than she'd expected.

"Angel?" Charlotte's voice cut into her thoughts and she brought her attention back to her own table.

"Uh-huh?" She tilted her head up and gave a little laugh. "Sorry, I must have been daydreaming."

She went back to talking with her friends, determined not to let things with Adam ruin this night out with them.

～

After seeing Angel and her friends in a booth at the pizzeria, Adam had left without even ordering the pepperoni pizza he'd been craving all day. Hungry and depressed, he'd slunk over to his sister Sarah's house. He stood on the porch, waiting for her to answer the door. The temperature was hovering just above freezing. Why, oh why had the groundhog seen its shadow? He didn't think he could take much more of the cold weather.

"Hey," Sarah said, opening the door. "Are you okay? You look awful."

"I feel awful." He followed her out of the cold and into the warm house.

As soon as they were inside, she hammered him with questions. "What's wrong? Are you sick? Does Mom know?"

"I'm not sick." He looked around the house. "Do you have any junk food?"

She eyed him. "Uh, I think I've got some tortilla chips. What's going on with you?"

"I messed up. There was this girl I was seeing and now she hates me."

"Whoa. Girl trouble?" She grabbed his arm. "Sit down. I want to hear more." She hurried out of the room and returned in a minute with a bag of tortilla chips and a bowl of salsa.

"So what happened? Why does she hate you? And how long were you dating? I don't remember you saying anything about dating anyone recently."

"Her name is Angel and she's new in town. Actually, her mom is from Candle Beach and she came here to find out more about her family."

"Okay, so what happened? Adam, get to the point!" She handed him a glass of wine.

Her eyes were popping out and her body seemed to be humming with impatience. Had it really been that long since he'd talked about dating anyone?

"She asked me to help her find her family and I agreed. Trouble is, I found her grandmother, Mary, and she didn't want me to tell Angel about her. I finally got her to agree to tell Angel herself, but until she does, I promised her I wouldn't say anything. Angel found out I'd been keeping a secret from her and now she wants nothing to do with me."

"Ouch. You really care about this girl, don't you?" Sarah eyed him from her perch on the arm of a chair. She stood to refill her wine glass, tipping the wine bottle toward him to ask if he would like more.

He nodded miserably. "Yes, and yes," he said nodding to the bottle. He sighed. "I haven't known her very long, but somehow I can imagine spending the rest of my life with her." Misery coursed throughout his veins. "She's beautiful and funny and smart and kind. A woman that I thought I'd never be able to find. And now I've lost her."

Sarah curled up in the chair, sipping her wine and gazing at him thoughtfully. "Adam, you're my brother, so don't let this go to your head, but you're actually quite a catch. Any woman would be lucky to have you."

"Thanks." He dropped his head into his hands and then glanced up at her. "Was I wrong to keep my promise to Mary?"

"I don't know."

"When I was talking with Mary, I could tell that she wanted to have a relationship with Angel, and I knew Angel wanted that more than anything. It seemed like the best thing to do was to honor Mary's wishes and not let Angel know about her until she was ready to do so herself." He leaned back against the cushions of the couch. "And now it's such a mess."

"I think it will all work out. She'll come to her senses and realize you didn't hurt her on purpose. Besides, at least you've been lucky enough to find the girl of your dreams. I don't think I'll ever find the right man for me, not here in Candle Beach."

He sat up. "Are you thinking about leaving? I feel like you just came back here."

"It's been a few years. For some reason I thought coming back to Candle Beach would feel like coming home, and it has been in some ways. I love being close by to see Mom and

Dad and you and Jenny and her kids. I feel like I missed out on seeing Charlie when he was a baby." She stood and paced the room. "But it's not the same as when I left. All my friends have moved away. They're all getting married and having kids, and here I am stuck in this small town, with not much chance of finding Mr. Right."

He stared at his sister, seeing her in a new light. He had no idea that she felt that way. Had he been so caught up in the newspaper and then lately with Angel that he'd ignored her?

"I'm sure you'll find someone. I mean, I thought the same thing until the day that Angel dropped my cherry Danish on the floor at the café." His voice caught, thinking about Angel.

A glimmer of a smile appeared on Sarah's face. "Is that how you met?"

"I haven't told you about that, have I?"

"No, I didn't even know about her until you showed up on my doorstep this evening, telling me that she's breaking up with you." She feigned a glare at her brother. "How is it that we have dinner with you every Sunday night and yet this is the first that I've heard about the mysterious Angel?"

He sighed. "I guess I have a lot on my mind." He grabbed a chip from the bowl that she had sat on the coffee table and dipped it into the ultra-hot salsa. Sarah was well known in the family for having a cast-iron stomach.

"Okay." She stared at him expectantly. "Are you going to tell me about how you met?"

"Oh yeah," he said sheepishly. He finished the chip that was covered in a generous amount of salsa, causing the roof of his mouth to burn. He slugged down some wine. "So, you know how I love getting some sort of donut or pastry in the mornings for breakfast?"

"Or for lunch or for a snack, or really any time of the day," she interjected.

He glared at her. "I'm not that bad. Anyway, Angel is the baker for the Bluebonnet Café, but she was filling in for the person at the cash register when I met her. There was one cherry Danish left, and I was so excited to get it because they were always out by the time I got in there. Somehow, the bag with the Danish fell to the floor when she was handing it to me, and there went my breakfast."

"I bet she felt bad."

He smiled, remembering how cute she'd been in her embarrassment.

"She did. She made extra for me the next morning, and said that she'd someday make me a full dozen." He slumped against the back of the couch. "So you're a woman, what do I do now?"

"Uh, you beg for forgiveness." She leaned forward, looking directly at him.

"But what if she won't talk to me again?"

"I'm willing to bet she'll talk to you, but if not, you're going to have to make some kind of grand gesture."

"Like in the movies?" He wrinkled his nose. "I don't think I have a boom box to blast love songs at her window."

"Adam, seriously?" Sarah shook her head. "How are men so dumb sometimes?"

Channeling his inner child, he stuck his tongue out at her. "That's what they do in the movies, right?" Then he sobered. "Seriously though, I don't know what I can do to make her forgive me."

"Well, you'd better figure it out. She's not going to wait forever."

He stood from the couch and stretched before putting

his coat on. "I'd better get home. Otis is probably wondering where I am. Thanks for everything."

"No problem, big brother." She followed him to the door and reached up to give him a hug. "It will work out, I promise."

"I hope so." He walked back out into the cold, shivering as he jammed his bare hands into his coat pockets. He hoped Sarah knew what she was talking about and that he could think of something to make Angel forgive him. At the moment, he didn't know what that would be.

17

*A*ngel came down the carriage house stairs at a few minutes after nine the next morning. Gretchen was leaning against her car, waiting for Angel. She made an exaggerated display of checking her watch.

"You only had to come downstairs. How are you late?" Gretchen teased.

Angel checked her own watch. "I'm only three minutes late." She'd been working on time management, but hadn't quite conquered it yet.

Gretchen peered at her. "How are you doing? You seemed really down last night." She hurried to add, "Not that I blame you."

"I'm okay. It's probably for the best. I need to focus on other things right now." She didn't know who she was trying to convince more, Gretchen or herself.

Gretchen eyed her critically, but didn't say anything.

"Really, I'm fine." She got into the car and shut the door.

"Okay." Gretchen shrugged as she sat in the driver's seat. "Let's get going then. We've got a lot of work to do."

The two of them had volunteered to put the newspaper

and pastry bundles together for that day. They'd need to see Adam to get the newspapers and Angel wasn't sure how she felt about seeing him again so soon after their breakup. But she'd made a commitment to help with the bundles and she didn't want to go back on her word.

Too soon, they were pulling up to the newspaper office.

Gretchen turned to her before getting out. "Are you sure you want to go in with me?"

"I'll be fine." No, she didn't want to go in there, but Gretchen couldn't carry all of the boxes out to the car by herself.

She followed her friend into the office, almost hiding behind her as they entered. Her pulse quickened, imagining having to talk with Adam. A few days ago, she'd been furious with him, and in the heat of the moment she'd said some things that she now regretted. Had she overreacted?

The office was empty and her worry seemed anti-climactic.

Where was Adam? The door was unlocked, so he had to be here. Anxiety over seeing him started to rear up.

"Hey," Adam said as he walked out of the back room. He stopped when he saw Angel. "Oh, I didn't expect to see you today."

She gave a tentative nod. "I said I'd help."

He pressed his lips together. "Thank you. I appreciate the help."

He almost looked like he was going to cry and her stomach twisted. She'd hurt him—something she'd never thought she'd do. But he'd hurt her first by not telling her the truth. He exited into the back room and she stared at him as he retreated. Should she tell him she was sorry about what she'd said?

Before she could decide, he brought out a dolly

containing the stacks of newspapers. "You asked for one hundred, right?"

Gretchen nodded. "Uh-huh. My parents said the trial run was so popular with the nightly rental guests that they want to roll it out to every guest."

"That's awesome," Angel said, turning to Gretchen. "I didn't know that." Even if a relationship between Adam and her hadn't worked out, she didn't want him to lose the newspaper.

"Do you need help with them?" he asked.

She and Gretchen exchanged glances and Angel shook her head.

"No, we're fine. Thanks." Gretchen grabbed the handle of the dolly, which was stacked high with newspapers.

Angel and Gretchen rolled the newspapers out and unloaded them into the trunk of the car. Angel could feel Adam's eyes on her through the office windows as she got into the passenger seat while Gretchen took the dolly back inside.

She leaned back against the seat. Seeing him hadn't been quite as bad as she'd expected, but she also hadn't thought much about how Adam would feel after the breakup.

~

If a grand gesture was needed to win Angel back, that was what he'd do. Adam took a moment to compose himself on Mary's front porch, then rapped on the door sharply. When she came to the door, she wore an expression of guilt and fear.

"Adam. I wasn't expecting to see you again." Her knuckles were white against the dark wood of the door.

"May I come inside?"

She glanced into the room. "Yes, come in."

He stood on a flowered rug near the entrance and took a steadying breath before addressing her.

"Mary. I need you to tell Angel that you're her grandmother."

Unless Mary told her the truth, Angel would never forgive him. Mary had promised that she'd tell her granddaughter who she was within two weeks, and now that time was almost up.

She sat down in an armchair in her small one-bedroom apartment, suddenly looking ten years older than she had when he'd first met her. She looked up at him.

"I can't do it." She shrank back down into the chair.

He closed his eyes. "What do you mean, you can't do it?"

She fiddled with the yarn fringe of a blue and green afghan, but said nothing.

He tried again. "Mary, you need to tell her."

She looked up, her eyes bright with tears. "I can't. What will she think of me?"

He sat down on the edge of the couch and leaned forward. "She'll think you're her grandmother."

"But I haven't seen her since she was three years old," she whispered.

"You made a mistake," he said firmly. "She's an adult now. A warm and caring adult. She'll understand." He hoped Angel would understand his reasons for keeping her grandmother's secret as well.

Her eyes drilled into his face. "She's special to you, isn't she? My granddaughter?"

"Yes." He stood and paced the room. "I hate keeping this a secret from her."

She nodded.

135

"I'm going to need to tell her tomorrow, whether you come with me or not."

"Alright." She took a deep breath. "I'll do it."

"You will?" He was almost afraid to hope. He didn't know if it would be enough to get Angel back, but at least she'd finally know her family.

"Yes." Her voice was shaky. "When should I tell her?"

He thought about it. He didn't want to take Mary to the Bluebonnet Café while Angel was working and he wasn't sure she'd open the door if he brought her grandmother to her house.

"The Sweethearts' Dance at the renovated Sorenson Farm barn. Angel is friends with Maggie Price and she'll be there. I know she will."

She nodded slowly. "I heard about it. I'm glad to see that the farm will be saved and won't become a new housing development. It's been around since before I was born." She stood. "I need a cup of tea. Would you like some?"

"No thanks."

She pushed herself up from the chair and busied herself in the kitchen before returning with a steaming cup of tea. "Do you think she'll agree to talk with me?"

"I don't know," he said honestly. At this point, Angel was pretty mad, but as far as she knew, Adam was the reason she hadn't yet met her grandmother. If he kept it that way, it might kill any chance for things between him and Angel, but if it saved her relationship with her family, it would be well worth it.

"I'll make it work." He met her gaze. "I'll pick you up tomorrow night at seven."

"Alright."

He turned to leave, but before he reached the door to see himself out, she called out to him.

"Adam."

He pivoted to face her.

"Thank you." Her hand shook as she set the tea cup down on the counter. "I'm sorry if this has caused problems with you and my granddaughter."

He pressed his lips together and nodded. "You're welcome."

Outside, he sat for a moment in his car and stared straight ahead. None of this had gone the way he wanted, but Angel was special and she deserved to know her grandmother and the rest of her family—even at the cost of his own happiness.

18

"Maggie, this is beautiful." The change from when Angel had been at the Sorenson Farm earlier in the week was astounding. While still rustic, the inside supports of the barn had been painted white and fairy lights hung from the rafters. The overall effect was that of a winter wonderland.

"No kidding," Dahlia said. "I had my doubts about your ability to pull this off, but I shouldn't have." Her eyes were wide as she took in the renovations. Beside her, her husband Garrett gestured that he was heading off toward the bar, and she nodded to him.

Gretchen slugged Dahlia's arm.

"Hey, I said I was wrong to doubt her."

Maggie glowed from the praise. "It's okay Dahlia, I had doubts too."

Jake came up behind his fiancé and put his arm around her. "I didn't. I knew you could pull it off." He kissed the top of her head and she snuggled into him.

Angel's stomach lurched watching the obvious love and affection between the two of them. She'd thought that she might have that with Adam, but she'd been proven wrong. Not that she shouldn't have expected that.

"Maggie, someone's asking for you over there." Jake pointed to a group of people at the back of the barn.

Maggie craned her head around to see who he was talking about, and her face lit up. "It's my parents and their friends. They haven't seen the place all done up yet."

"Go, go." Dahlia motioned for her to leave and the two of them walked away.

When the happy couple was out of earshot, she nudged Angel. "Why so glum?" She scanned the room. "Did Adam come with you, or is he coming later? Garrett almost didn't make it because he has a deadline on his newest novel, but luckily he finished up in time."

Gretchen hissed, "Dahlia."

"What?" Dahlia looked back and forth between her two friends. "Did I miss something?"

Angel stared at the ground. "He's not coming to the dance—at least not with me."

"What happened?" Dahlia asked. "I thought you two were an item now."

"We broke up."

Dahlia gasped. "Why? I thought things were going so well."

Angel looked longingly at the exit. "I thought so too until I found out that he'd been keeping the identity of my family a secret from me."

"Seriously?" Dahlia asked. "I can't believe Adam would do that." She shook her head. "It doesn't seem like him, but I guess you never really know people." She turned to Gretchen. "Do you think Adam would lie to Angel?"

Gretchen's face reddened and she spoke as though she were choosing her words very carefully. "I don't think he would lie to anyone unless he had a really good reason for doing so."

"Well, he did." Angel jutted out her chin. "He told me so himself." She scanned Gretchen's face. "You knew, didn't you?"

Gretchen hung her head. "I did. I'm so sorry, Angel. And Adam is sorry too. This has been eating him up since he found out."

"Well, why was he lying to me then? I can handle it if my family doesn't want to see me or whatever." She toed the wooden planks lightly with the sole of her shoe, then stared at Gretchen and Dahlia, who now looked like they'd rather be anywhere but where they were. "You know, never mind. Just the fact that he lied to me is enough to make me know that he isn't the right guy for me. And I can't believe you didn't tell me either. I thought we were friends."

"But Angel—let him explain," Gretchen pled.

Angel tossed her hair back. "I'm getting a drink now. This is supposed to be a dance, right? We should be having fun, not talking about the man who did me wrong, like I was the star of a country western song."

"I'll come with you. Garrett's still over there too." Dahlia grabbed her arm and walked with her over to the line for the bar.

As they waited for their drinks, Angel snuck a peek at Gretchen. She was now leaning against one of the barn walls, biting her lip as though trying to hold back tears. At that moment, Parker came in and made a beeline to where his girlfriend was standing. Gretchen immediately crumpled into him. Parker glanced over to Angel and Dahlia and then put his arm around Gretchen, leading her outside. Dahlia had her back to them and didn't see the exchange, but Angel's heart sank. She hadn't meant to hurt her friend and she knew Gretchen hadn't meant to hurt her either.

After they got their drinks, Dahlia set hers down on one of the round tables set up along the exterior wall of the barn and joined Garrett on the dance floor. Angel sat down, sipping her Merlot and watching her friends swirl happily around the dance floor with their partners. Maggie's face was flushed as she and Jake danced by and she appeared to be having the time of her life.

Angel had actually been looking forward to going to this dance with Adam. She'd even bought a new dress especially for the occasion. Now, seeing how happy her friends were, she couldn't take it anymore. She reached down to the floor to pick up her purse, but when her head emerged from under the table skirts, she realized she wasn't alone.

Adam stood next to the table, wearing a nicely tailored black suit. He looked incredibly handsome, but Angel fought to push that thought away. There was no future for her with him.

"I was just leaving." She held up her purse to show him and stood from the table.

He put his hand on her arm, his touch causing her stomach to flutter. "Please don't go."

"I wasn't having much fun anyway. It's not because you're here." She pushed her chair in and then hesitated, waiting to see how he would respond.

He took a deep breath. "Angel, I truly am sorry. I didn't want to lie to you."

She looked up at him. "Then why did you?"

"I did find out who your grandmother is. But she made me promise not to tell you—at least not yet."

She folded her arms over her chest. "Okay, so who is she? Are you able to tell me now?" Even if he'd promised her grandmother that he wouldn't tell her who she was, it still didn't make things right.

He held up a finger. "Wait."

She narrowed her eyes at him. She was giving him a chance to explain himself, and now he was walking away from her? "Never mind." She walked quickly toward the exit. The sound of hurried footsteps followed her, and she quickened her pace.

"Angel, wait."

She stopped and whirled around. Adam's momentum caused him to crash into her, and she wobbled on her high heels. Before she could go down, he caught her by the waist, stabilizing her. Her skin burned where his fingers rested on the thin fabric of her dress. Caught off guard, she stared at him.

"What do you want?"

"Please don't go yet. I need to show you something, or rather someone." He peered into her eyes. "I know you don't have any reason to trust me, but can you wait here for me? Just for a minute, I promise."

She nodded and he strode off toward the barn door. Thoughts swirled in her mind. Why should she listen to him? And what was he talking about? Now didn't seem like the appropriate time to meet new people—she wasn't in the mood for it. She was just about to continue on her way home when Adam returned with an older woman in tow.

The woman hung back, but seemed to be assessing her. An odd sensation traveled up her spine. Was this her grandmother? There was something familiar about her, although Angel wasn't sure whether it was the slight resemblance to her mother, or perhaps from a long-ago memory.

She looked at Adam for an introduction, and he put his hand on the woman's arm.

"Mary, this is your granddaughter, Angel." He turned to Angel. "And this is your grandmother, Mary Thomason." His gaze alternated between the two of them.

Neither of the women spoke for a moment. Angel stared into her eyes, the same blue eyes that both she and her mother had inherited. This was her grandmother. She didn't know what to say or feel.

"It's nice to meet you." She held her hand out tentatively and Mary shook it limply. She was trembling like a frightened rabbit.

"It's nice to meet you too, Angel."

"Well, I think the two of you have a lot to talk about. Maybe we could go sit down over at that table?" Adam pointed at the empty table where Angel had been sitting when he arrived.

Angel glanced at her grandmother and then back to Adam. At this point, what did she have to lose? She nodded, and they followed Adam over to the table. Angel and her grandmother took chairs that were several seats apart. Adam sat across from them, as if wanting to stay out of the reunion but be close enough in case they needed him.

Angel and Mary stared at each other, unsure of how to start.

"So you're my grandmother," Angel said slowly.

Mary nodded. "Yes." She took a deep breath. "You have no idea how much I've been wanting to meet you. You've grown into such a beautiful woman."

Angel bit her lip and stared down into her lap. "Thank you." She brought her head up and peered at her grandmother. "Why did you never contact me? My mother and I were all alone in Los Angeles, with no other family around. You knew about us. You knew about me. Did you not care about me?"

Mary's face crumbled and tears streamed down her face. "I wanted to see you. Please believe me, I did." She plucked a Kleenex out of her purse and dabbed at her face.

"Then why? Why didn't you come see me?" Angel was getting angry now. This woman, her grandmother, had known about her all these years and yet hadn't bothered to make contact with her.

"Your grandfather was a strict man." Mary clutched her purse tightly in her lap. "When your mother became pregnant at sixteen and refused to tell us who the father was, he was furious. After you were born, you and Erin lived with us for a few years, but he could never forgive her, and it caused a rift between them. Erin finally had enough and took you away. I didn't even know where you had gone."

"But you didn't look for us." How could her grandmother have known she was alive and not even bother to look?

"I know," Mary whispered. Fresh tears appeared in her eyes. "Your grandfather was a very controlling man, and he ordered me not to make contact with Erin or you. He said it was your mother's choice to leave."

"But what about after he died? Couldn't you have come looking for us then?"

"I could have. But I didn't. That will be my greatest regret that I keep with me until my dying day." Mary leaned forward, reaching her hand out along the table toward Angel. "If you will let me, I would like to be a part of your life now." In a small voice, she added, "But if you want nothing to do with me, I will understand."

Angel didn't know what to think. She'd finally found her grandmother, but then learned that the woman had known about her all along and never tried to find her. Did she really want someone like that in her life? She looked back at the old woman.

"If you'll excuse me, I would like to get some air." She rose from her chair, rushing toward the barn door as quickly as she could without tripping in her heels. When she stopped at the door to look back, Adam had moved from his chair and was now sitting next to Mary, his head close to hers as if consoling her.

She leaned against the outside of the barn, gazing out toward Bluebonnet Lake but not really seeing it. She had a grandmother, right here in Candle Beach. Someone who had known about her for her entire life but had done nothing about it. And now she wanted Angel to forgive her and pretend like nothing had happened? How was that even possible? Too many years had gone by.

But wasn't this what she wanted? She'd gone into this knowing that she may discover something she didn't want to find. And her grandmother didn't seem like a complete monster—just a scared old woman. In truth, it sounded like it had been her grandfather who had been the reason for her mother to flee from Candle Beach when Angel was young. But that still didn't completely excuse her grandmother from disowning them as well.

She pushed away from the barn wall and walked down the slight incline to the dock that stuck out into the lake. A slight breeze caused the water to ripple in places, the moonlight highlighting its shimmering surface. What was the alternative here? What would she do if she didn't accept her grandmother's apology? Was there a future for her here in Candle Beach?

There were things that she loved about this beautiful town—her job at the Bluebonnet Café, the easy access to the ocean, and the friendly townspeople who had welcomed her into their arms. However, if she stayed, there would always be the ghost of a possibility of romance between her and Adam. And what would it be like to live in a town where she knew that her grandmother lived only a few blocks away and yet have no relationship with her?

She sat down on the rough boards of the dock, taking care not to tear her dress, and pulled her knees up to her chest. It was even cooler down here than it had been up by the barn, and she fervently wished that she had remembered to grab her coat on the way out. She hugged her legs and gazed out at the lake, allowing its beauty to draw her in. Was this what she wanted her future to look like? Living a lonely life when she'd been offered the chance to have a family nearby, the family that she'd always hoped to have.

She stood carefully and hiked back up the slope to the barn. Adam was waiting for her next to the door. He must've been watching her as she sat down by the lake. He tried to talk to her as she brushed past him, but she wasn't ready to speak with him yet. For now, she had something else to do.

She approached her grandmother tentatively. The older woman had her hands wrapped around a mug of coffee, looking wistfully out at the dancers, much as Angel had done earlier.

"Mary? Grandmother?"

The woman turned slowly, tears coming to her eyes when she saw Angel standing next to her. "Yes?"

"I'm sorry, I don't know what to call you." Angel sat down next to her at the table.

"That's okay. I'm hoping that you will eventually call me Grandmother, but I'll take anything. Please, please let me have a chance to get to know you. A chance to make things right with you." She pressed her lips together, her eyes pleading.

Angel took a deep breath. "Okay. I'd like to try." She reached for her water glass on the table. "Let's start with something easy. Did my mother have a sister?"

Mary's face lit up. "Yes, her name is Rilla. She has two daughters, one who's a senior in high school, and another who is fifteen. They are wonderful girls. I think you'll really like them." She hesitated. "And I think they'll like you too."

"Do they know about me?" It seemed odd to think that she had two cousins that she knew nothing about, and hadn't even known existed prior to two minutes ago.

"Yes, Rilla has told them about you. When Erin moved away, she was so angry at my husband that she broke off contact with everyone in the family. Rilla was heartbroken. I think she never quite forgave her father and me for causing her big sister to leave."

So her aunt was on her mother's side. "I'd love to get to know her too." A rush of love came over her. She had a family—people who had known her mother and had loved her. A grandmother and aunt, even cousins to get to know. A tear dripped down her face and she swiped it away with the back of her hand. "When can I meet everyone?"

Mary smiled and took her hand. "I'll call Rilla tomorrow morning and set something up."

Angel nodded. "I'd like that."

Mary hugged her and whispered, "Thank you for giving me a chance."

a draft rippled the papers on Adam's desk. He looked up from his computer and his heart lifted. Angel. He hadn't expected to see her here again.

"Hi." He stood from his desk and walked around to the other side, afraid to get too close to her. She wore a turquoise shirt over blue jeans, nothing fancy, but she would be beautiful in anything.

"Hi," she said tentatively.

"Donuts?" He leaned against the edge of his desk, and gestured to the white box she held in her hands.

She looked down at it, then met his eyes. "No. They're 'I'm sorry' Danishes."

A smile spread across his lips. "Cherry?"

She grinned back at him. "Yes." She opened the box to reveal a dozen cherry Danishes.

He lifted his eyebrows. "You must have thought I was really hungry."

"Aren't you always?" she teased.

He glared at her. "Funny."

Her mood turned serious. "I really am sorry. I know you

were only keeping my grandmother a secret because she asked you to."

He closed his eyes for a moment. "I felt horrible keeping it from you."

"I know." She put the pastries down on his desk and came closer to him. The scent of gardenias floated in the air, making his office reminiscent of a flower garden. His pulse increased with every step she took. When she was about a foot away, she halted.

He reached his fingers out to tentatively touch her hand. "I missed you."

"I missed you too." Angel smiled and threaded her fingers through his. She peered into his eyes. "Don't ever lie to me again though, okay?"

He pulled her closer. "I'll never lie to you, but with my career, there may be things that I'm not able to tell you."

She flinched and his heart stopped. Was that a deal breaker?

She took a deep breath. "I can live with that."

"Good." He ran his hand up the curve of her neck and cupped her head behind her ears, caressing her silky hair with his thumb and forefinger. It still amazed him how quickly she'd become such an integral part of his life.

She sighed and put her hands on his shoulders. Taking it as an invitation, he bent his head and kissed her softly on the lips. She closed her eyes and sank into him.

After a moment, he lowered his hands to her upper arms and gazed into her eyes. "I know we haven't been in each other's lives for long, but I feel like we've known each other forever. When you weren't talking to me, it felt like a part of me was missing." He searched her face, hoping she felt the same way.

She smiled at him, her eyes glistening with happy tears.

"It was hard for me too. I've never had that with anyone else before, so I knew what we had was special."

Adam's heart swelled with joy and he pulled her close again, never wanting to let her go. Being here with her was worth everything they'd gone through to arrive at this moment and he couldn't wait to see what the future would bring for the two of them.

∽

Butterflies fluttered in Angel's stomach as she stood outside Off the Vine. It had been two days since the Sweethearts' Dance on Valentine's Day and this was the first time she'd seen everyone since then. Gretchen would be there and she felt horrible about the way she'd treated her friend at the dance. She knew Gretchen had been caught in the middle between Adam and Angel as they worked through the secrecy over her grandmother. Would she be mad? She didn't want to lose Gretchen's friendship, and as her tenant, it would make things awkward if they weren't on good speaking terms.

She took a deep breath and entered the dimly lit restaurant. The other women had managed to snag the prime corner booth, which was big enough to seat everyone in their growing crowd. Dahlia, Maggie, and Gretchen were already there.

Dahlia eyed Angel. "Well, you look a lot happier than the last time I saw you." Maggie and Gretchen nodded.

"I am." Angel looked around the wine bar. It was weird how everything seemed so much brighter now that she wasn't carrying around so many heavy emotions. Gretchen didn't look too mad—in fact, she'd never looked so happy.

"Did everything turn out okay between you and Adam?" Gretchen asked.

Angel smiled. "It did." Her expression fell. "And I'm so sorry about how I treated you. I shouldn't have taken my anger out on you."

Gretchen leaned over and gave her a quick hug. "It's okay. I know you didn't mean it, and I felt bad not telling you too. Adam was miserable about not telling you, so I'm glad you forgave him. He deserves a second chance."

Angel turned to Maggie. "And I ran out of the dance without complimenting you on how lovely everything was. I have to admit, I had my doubts, but the barn was gorgeous."

"Thanks. I was pretty happy with it too. And it seems like other people in town liked what we've done with the place. We've already had several inquiries about booking events there in the coming months."

"Did I miss anything else?" She glanced from friend to friend. They all wore mischievous grins.

"Oh, maybe just a little," Charlotte said, coming up behind her with a huge grin on her face. She put her hand on Gretchen's shoulder. "Gretchen? Do you have anything to show Angel?" She slid into the booth next to Angel, staring pointedly at Gretchen.

Gretchen blushed, but held up her left hand, revealing a beautiful sparking diamond.

Angel's eyes widened. "Parker proposed?"

"Yes. On Valentine's Day, at the dance. Cheesy, right?" Her cheeks glowed with the happiness that cosmetics manufacturers tried so hard to emulate.

"Maybe a little, but I'm so happy for you. Besides, that ring makes up for it." She grabbed Gretchen's hand to examine the ring closer.

"Yeah, my brother's finally settling down." Charlotte laughed when Gretchen glared at her. "And I couldn't be more happy about it." She grinned goofily at her future sister-in-law.

"Enough about me." Gretchen waved her hand in the air.

"Well, I have some news." Dahlia looked around at them. "Garrett and I are thinking about taking a several-month-long trip to Europe. I've never been and since we want to have kids soon, we figured now would be a good time."

Maggie smiled and rubbed her hands together. "Ooh. It'll be so nice to have a friend who has children too."

"Hey, what are the rest of us, chopped liver?" Gretchen asked.

"No, but having kids changes you. You always have to consider their needs when making a decision. Even going out for drinks with friends can become a logistical nightmare." Maggie made a face. "I'm glad Jake and Alex get along so well."

"Yeah, when's your wedding?" Angel grinned at her boss. If she was going to be part of this group, she wanted to join in on the good-natured teasing that seemed rampant among them.

"As soon as possible—my apartment lease is up soon and I can't wait to move into the farmhouse. Oh, and Jake's a pretty good reason too," Maggie joked. "Seriously though, with the barn renovations, I haven't had much time to think about it. Maybe we'll have a double wedding with Gretchen and Parker."

Gretchen's eyebrows shot up. "Um...we haven't really planned it out yet."

"I'm kidding!" Maggie took a big sip of her Pinot Gris.

"We want a quiet ceremony, with just family and a few friends. Of course, all of you will be invited."

"What about you?" Angel asked Charlotte. "I heard you have a painting in an exhibition in Seattle."

Charlotte's eyes lit up. "I do. They took one of my ocean scenes. It starts in a few weeks."

"That's amazing," Angel said.

"I know. I've been trying for years to get noticed. I'm hoping this is my big break."

"I knew you could do it." Maggie held up her glass. "Here's a toast to all of us. May our success continue."

They all toasted and cheered so loudly that more than a few of the other customers turned to stare at them. Angel cheekily tipped her glass at the onlookers. They smiled and went back to their own business.

20

_____

*A*ngel stared at the yellow house with trepidation. This was it. She was finally going to meet her aunt and cousins. Beyond the front door of the house from the photo, were people she was related to—people that she hoped would someday love her and consider her a part of their family.

She took a deep breath and unbuckled her seatbelt.

"Are you sure you don't need to be working?" She peered into his eyes. "I appreciate you coming with me, but I don't want to take up all your time." She tilted her head to the side. "Hey, how's that article on the logging industry going?"

Adam seemed to freeze. "Uh, it's going." He stared out the window.

He'd been so excited about it before, what was going on?

"Did you get good information from that guy you interviewed?"

He stepped out of the car. "I didn't meet with him."

"Wait, why not?" She got out of the car and stood next to the hood of the car, staring at him.

"It just didn't work out." He toed the ground with the tip of his shoe.

"I feel like you aren't telling me the whole truth. You promised not to hide things from me, remember?"

He sighed. "You're right. I didn't end up meeting with John Nichols because that was the day I met your grandmother instead."

A cold wave slammed into her. "You gave up your interview for me?" she whispered.

"Eh." Adam shrugged. "I'm sure I wouldn't have gotten very good information from him anyways. It's not a big deal."

"Right." She looked at him sideways. He may not be lying to her anymore, but he was hiding how he felt. Her stomach twisted. That interview would have been major for him and his news article.

He reached over and wrapped his arm around her shoulders. "Don't worry about it. New opportunities will come up, okay?"

"Okay," she said, although she wasn't convinced. But for now, there wasn't anything she could do about his missed interview and she needed to focus on meeting her aunt and cousins for the first time. "Adam," she whispered.

"Yeah?" He stopped to look at her. "Is something wrong?"

"No. I don't know." She glanced up at the house again. "What if they don't like me?"

She'd already determined her family weren't monsters, but there was still the possibility that they wouldn't accept her. As much as she loved her mother, Erin Bennett's decision had kept Angel from them for so many years.

"They'll love you. Don't worry about it." He reached out for her hand and squeezed it.

The front door opened, revealing a woman in her late thirties. Two teenaged girls crowded around behind her, sticking their heads out to catch a glimpse of their new cousin.

"Angel?" the woman said hesitantly.

Angel nodded and walked closer, breaking apart from Adam.

"I'm your aunt, Rilla." Tears streamed down her face and she ran down the steps to hug Angel. "You look just like your mother," her aunt said, scanning her face. "I can't believe it."

Angel wrapped her arms around her aunt, her eyes filling with tears of her own. The embrace was warm and comforting, even better than she'd imagined it would be.

"Mom, we want to meet her too!" one of the girls said. Her other cousin nodded as she braced herself on the door frame.

Rilla pulled away from Angel and put her arm around her niece's shoulders. "Let's go inside. I've made us a nice quiche for lunch, if that's okay with you." She glanced at Adam. "And you must be Adam."

"Yes." He nodded and walked closer to her. "Nice to meet you."

"Nice to meet you too. My mother has told me about how you helped bring Angel together with our family." Rilla's eyes misted over again. "I can't even tell you how much it means to me."

Adam smiled. "I'm happy to help. It means a lot to me for Angel to meet you too."

Rilla beckoned for them to follow her inside. A sense of familiarity came over Angel as she entered the house she'd wondered about for so long.

"Do you remember this house?" Rilla asked. "I

remember when you were just a toddler, playing with the pots and pans from the drawer under the stove." She gestured across the room at the stove.

Angel's gaze followed her aunt's hand and she was flooded with memories. "My mom used to sing to me and let me beat on the pots with a wooden spoon while she sang."

Rilla laughed. "That drove my father nuts, but I always thought it was funny." She hugged Angel, then opened the refrigerator, pulling out a carton of strawberries and a bottle of cream. The aroma of a vegetable and bacon laden quiche filled the air.

Angel's cousins hovered around the kitchen table and Rilla turned to them. "Girls, why don't you go work on homework. I'll call you when lunch is ready, okay?"

"But Mom..." the older girl whined.

Rilla fixed her eyes on her daughters and they hustled out of the room. She motioned for Angel and Adam to sit down at the table.

"Do you want some coffee?" Rilla asked, holding a mug near the coffee pot.

They both nodded. "Yes please."

Rilla set two cups of coffee down on the table, along with a cutting board. She picked up a paring knife and with the flip of her wrist, sliced off the top of a strawberry, neatly cutting it into even portions.

Angel sipped her coffee, trying to come up with something to say to her aunt.

Rilla broke the silence first. "I knew your mom had gone to Los Angeles. She sent me a postcard when she first got down there, letting me know you were both okay."

Angel stared at her. "So why didn't you contact us?"

Her aunt studied the strawberry she held in one hand. "I didn't want to cross my father and I was only in middle school. I had no way of getting down there to see the two of you. After I graduated from high school, I attended college in California, hoping to see her. But when I located the return address from the postcard, you'd already moved."

"We moved a lot when I was a little kid." Angel rubbed her finger along the handle of the ceramic mug. "Until my mother met my stepfather, we didn't have much money."

Rilla covered Angel's hand with hers. "It must have been very difficult for her, being a single mother of a young child." She shook her head. "I can't even imagine."

Tears formed in the corners of Angel's eyes. "She was a wonderful mother."

Rilla looked down at her lap. "I miss my big sister. I wish I'd stood up to my father. I know Mom does too."

Angel stood and leaned over to hug her aunt. "I'm sure my mother understood."

From the doorway, one of her cousins cleared her throat. "Is it time for lunch yet? We're starving."

Rilla glanced at the timer. "Just about. Why don't you girls get washed up and set the table."

"Oh, I can do that," Angel said.

"No, no." Rilla gestured to the table. "You're our guest. You don't need to help."

"I'm not a guest." Angel grinned as she pulled plates down from a cabinet with glass doors. "I'm family."

Rilla bit her lower lip and her eyes were misty. "Yes. You are."

During lunch, Angel kept taking surreptitious glances around the table. Family. She had a family again. Coming to Candle Beach had been a leap of faith, but it had paid off.

After eating, they chatted for a while in the living room until Rilla realized she was late for a church commitment.

"I'm so sorry, Angel. I'd love to stay here with you all day. It's been almost like having my sister here with me again."

"I know the feeling." Being around her aunt had helped fill the void that her mother's death had left. If only her mother had been able to see her mother and sister again and meet her nieces. She would have loved the woman her little sister had become. "I'll call you later, okay? Maybe we can get together for dinner later this week."

"I'd like that." Rilla put her coat on and they walked to the door together. "And Angel? Thank you for giving us a chance." She turned to Adam. "It was wonderful to meet you too."

He nodded. "Thank you for lunch. I'm happy Angel had the opportunity to meet you."

"I'm so glad I found you. Bye, Aunt Rilla." Angel hugged her aunt again, then waved goodbye and she and Adam walked down the street to her car.

~

The next day, Angel burst into the newspaper office. Adam glanced up in surprise.

"I thought you had to work."

"I did. I mean, I am working." She sighed. "Maggie said it was okay for me to come down here for a few minutes."

A slow smile spread over his face. "Well, I'm glad you did." He got up and kissed her gently. "Are you able to stay for lunch? We could grab Chinese takeout."

She shook her head. "I can't. I only came down here because I wanted to tell you that according to Maggie, John Nichols comes in for an afternoon coffee break almost every afternoon around two."

"Good for him. He's a busy man and he deserves to take

some time off to relax." Adam cocked his head to the side. "But why are you telling me this?"

She sighed in exasperation. "Because, he's there alone every afternoon. If you just happened to be there at the same time..."

"Maybe he'd be willing to talk with me about his deal with the timber company," Adam finished. He gave her a giant bear hug. "Angel, you're a genius."

She flushed. "I don't know about that, but I figured you could probably charm your way into a meeting with him. After all, you do share a love of coffee and sweets."

He grinned. Angel knew him well. "Thank you." He cast a frenzied glance around the office. "I've got so much to do if I'm going to talk with him today."

She laughed. "I've got to get back to work." She turned to leave, calling over her shoulder, "good luck!"

21

*A*ngel peered anxiously at Adam as they drove to his parents' house. "Are you sure your mother will like me?"

He smiled. "You wondered the same thing about your aunt and she adores you. Don't worry. Mom and Dad are going to love you."

"I hope so." She'd never been in a serious enough relationship before to meet her boyfriend's parents, so this was all new to her. And for her first time meeting them to be at a Sunday family dinner—well, that just wasn't fair. "Maybe we could do this a different day."

He reached across the center console and covered her hands with his right hand. "It will be fine, stop worrying so much."

She sat back in the passenger seat. He drove down a street not too far away from where her Aunt Rilla lived and parallel parked outside a green rambler.

"This is it." He came around to her side and opened the door. "They don't bite."

She took his hand and he led her up the cement walkway.

A woman came to the door before they'd even had a chance to ring the doorbell.

"You must be Angel!" She enveloped Angel in a big hug.

Angel's limbs felt like they were made of wood, hanging awkwardly down by her sides. The woman, who had hair the same carrot-red as Adam's, didn't seem to notice.

"I'm Sally," she said after she released Angel. "Adam's mother. "Come in, come in. Everyone's here—well, except Sarah." She motioned for them to follow her down the hall. A child's shriek echoed down the hallway. "They're all excited to meet you," she called over her shoulder.

Angel exchanged a glance with Adam and he shrugged.

"You're the first girl I've ever brought home." He flashed her a grin, holding her hand as they walked down the hallway.

She took a deep breath and tried to focus on him and how much he meant to her. Meeting his family was big. *No pressure, Angel.*

In the living room, a woman and man in their thirties sat next to each other on the couch. Two small children ran around the room, the little girl chasing the older boy. An older man rose from his chair and held out his hand to Angel.

"I'm Del, Adam's father. It's good to meet you." He leaned in closer and whispered, "And don't let us intimidate you. Sally will probably be full of questions."

Angel nodded. "Thanks," she whispered back.

After Adam introduced her to Jenny and Rick and the kids, his mother announced dinner was ready.

"Are we waiting for Sarah?" Jenny asked, glancing out the living room window.

"No, she said she'd be a little late and to start without us." Sally came out of the kitchen holding a large roasted chicken in a pan. She set it down on a trivet on the table and removed the potholders from her hands. "Sit, everyone, sit." She exited to the kitchen to get the rest of the food. As soon as his mother was out of the room, Adam disobeyed her and went into the kitchen to help her carry out the food.

Angel sat near one end of the table, next to where Adam had been sitting. After everyone was seated and ready to eat, a woman in her late twenties came in.

"Sorry I'm late, everyone." She noticed Angel and introduced herself as she slid into the empty chair. "You must be Angel. I'm Sarah."

"Nice to meet you, Sarah."

Angel looked down at her full plate. Around her everyone was chattering about things that had happened during the week. For someone unused to big families, it was a little overwhelming.

"Are you okay?" Adam asked, nudging her with his shoulder.

"Yes." She smiled weakly. "Just getting used to everyone." She lifted her head to look at everyone. Across the table, Sarah grinned at her, and Angel could instantly tell that they'd be friends.

"So, Angel. Adam tells me you're from California. Have you been in Candle Beach for long?" Sally asked.

"Oh, about two months." She ate a bite of chicken.

"Have you and Adam been dating long?" Sally leaned forward to hear her answer. "Adam doesn't tell us much about his personal life."

"We've been together about a month."

"A month?" Sally stared accusingly at her son.

"Yes, Mom." Adam wiped his mouth. "I didn't want to scare her off earlier by telling her all about you guys."

"Hey." Sarah smiled at Angel again. "Let's give them a break. Adam brought her to dinner to meet you now."

"Thanks, Sarah," Adam said.

Del cleared his throat. "Adam, how is your story on the logging industry going? Your mother said you'd made some progress lately."

Adam smiled at Angel. "Yes, thanks to Angel, I was able to secure an interview with John Nichols about his plans to sell the timber rights for some of his acreage. The article will be out in next week's edition of the *Candle Beach Weekly*."

"That's wonderful," Jenny said. "I'm looking forward to reading it."

They all started chattering again, and this time Angel did her best to follow the conversation, which ranged from school to work to the logging industry's effects on the town. It amazed her how much they all knew about each other's lives. No wonder they were upset that Adam had kept her a secret. It was hard to imagine living in a family like this where everyone shared things. Would she ever have that with her grandmother and aunt?

She'd enjoyed getting to know Rilla and her cousins. Eventually, she hoped to have a real relationship with all of her family in Candle Beach. For now, she wasn't going to push it. She looked over at Adam. She planned to stay in Candle Beach for the foreseeable future, and there would be time to get to know the members of her mother's family.

After they finished eating, Sally invited everyone to stay for a game of Pictionary. Adam demurred, saying Angel needed to get home. Angel was about to protest that she didn't have to work the next day, but then thought better of it. As great as his family was, she wasn't used to being around so many people at once and she needed some down time.

Outside the house, Adam squeezed her hand. "See, I told you they'd love you."

"I really liked them too. Your sisters are great."

He made a face. "Yeah, most of the time."

She laughed. Seeing the gentle jesting between him and his sisters had made her wish even more than before that she'd had a sibling.

He looked into her eyes. "Do you want to grab Otis and go for a walk on the beach?"

"Yes," she said. "That sounds perfect." Somehow, he'd known exactly what she needed—a quiet walk on the beach.

They drove back to his apartment and parked. Otis heard them coming up the stairs in the newspaper office and barked a few times.

"Yeah, yeah. We're here to spring you," Adam said as he ruffled the dog's fur and attached his leash.

When they got to the beach, there were a few people out for a post-dinner stroll. They held hands, walking together on the sand with Otis running out in front of them.

"This is nice. A perfect way to spend a Sunday evening." She gazed out at the ocean. The sun was a ball of fire, slipping behind the horizon and leaving a trail of oranges and pinks behind it.

"You mean you didn't like dinner at my parents' house?" Adam asked.

Her eyes widened. "No, that's not what I meant. It's just that…"

"They can be a bit much." He finished her sentence. "I

often feel the same way. But they're my family and I wouldn't change them for anything."

"I'm sure I'll get used to them."

"You'd better," he teased. "I plan for you to be at many more Sunday dinners in the future."

"I'd like that." She turned and put her hands on his chest, looking into his eyes. "Thank you again for finding my family. It means a lot to me."

He kissed the top of her head. "Me too. I want Candle Beach to feel like home to you."

She moved her hands up to his neck and kissed his lips. "It already does, because you're here."

His eyes met hers. "I never thought I'd say this to anyone so soon, but it feels like I've known you forever. Angel Bennett, I love you."

"I love you too," she said softly.

He smiled and pulled her snugly against him. She closed her eyes and rested her head on his chest, feeling safe and loved. Family, friends, and a new love. Candle Beach *was* home.

<<<<>>>>

THANK YOU FOR READING SWEET MEMORIES!

I hope you enjoyed Angel's story. If you did, please leave a review on Amazon. I would really appreciate it! Reviews are a huge factor in a book's success and I'd love to write more in this series.

For information about my new releases, please sign up for my newsletter at my website, www.nicoleellisauthor.com

Thank You,

Nicole

Candle Beach Sweet Romances

Dahlia's Story: Sweet Beginnings

Gretchen's Story: Sweet Success

Maggie's Story: Sweet Promises

Jill Andrews Cozy Mysteries

Brownie Points for Murder

Death to the Highest Bidder (coming April 16th)

Thank you for reading Sweet Memories!

A Deadly Pair O'Docks (coming May 15th)

Available on Amazon and Kindle Unlimited

ACKNOWLEDGMENTS

Editing by Free Bird Editing and LaVerne Clarke Editing
Cover Design by Mariah Sinclair

CPSIA information can be obtained
at www.ICGtesting.com
Printed in the USA
LVHW091516040921
696958LV00020B/590

9 781980 898757